I0658251

Tales of

Wudgi Crossing

Tall Tales of a Short Town

David.Lewis.Paget

BARR BOOKS

For Lyn...
for putting up with me for twenty eight years,
and not complaining more than once or twice a
day...

The characters in these pages are fictitious,
and are not intended to depict any living
person. Accordingly, if any reader should spot
any of these characters on the road, they have
my permission to run them over.

Beware!

Do not read this book unless you are mentally stable and physically fit. The author and publisher accept no responsibility for medical bills relating to ruptured spleens, incontinent bladders or psychiatric disorders arising as a result of ingesting the contents of these pages.

This is not a novel, it is a black comedy, a series of stories with a common backdrop, the streets and swamps of Wudgi Crossing. This tiny South Australian town may be searched for unstintingly through the pages of any Gazetteer, the Mobil Series of South Australian Maps, or the murky depths of Arabella Silkenshanks hot nourishing broth. It will not be found.

Indeed, up to and including the present day, the South Australian Government has always blamed Wudgi Crossing on Victoria, or New South Wales, or Zacariah Cribb's great-grandfather who took a left instead of a right at Moonee Ponds, and basically opened up the whole Pandora's Box. But the real culprits were Mick McGurk and his mate Jack Turnip, the latter of whom has a statue to his memory, sitting in a horse trough with a bucket on his head. So you can see what you're letting yourself in for....

Contents

Too Many Ducks   7

Harry's Homecoming   23

The Guided Tour   38

A Question of Anastasia   51

The Witching Wars of Wudgi   62

The Funeral of Zacariah Cribb   74

The Devereaux of Dingbat Mansions   84

The Rustik Flok Concert   96

The Wudgi Tram   109

McSoufflé and the Flying Saucer   130

A Gruesome Interlude   150

Hot, Nourishing Broth   166

Hong Kong Flu   178

Toad in the Hall   185

Cora Littledove's Main Chance   209

Wallywools and the Pigfest   221

Too Many Ducks

Down in a hollow by an old creek bed, somewhere to the north of South Australia, lies a dysfunctional township called Wudgi Crossing. Slandered and libelled over the years, misreported, lost, omitted from the great survey of 1888, and again from the Gazetteer of 1927, Wudgi Crossing is still the sort of outback town that you stumble across by accident - if you happen to be that unlucky.

It was actually a cattle crossing in the 1860's, a place you had to go through, rather than either leave from or arrive at. At the bottom of the hill ran a creek - or as is the way with Australian creeks, didn't run a creek. For most of the year it was dry, only consenting to dampen its banks during the winter, when the great flood of waters flowed down from a distant mountain range. Nevertheless, it was handy, this dry creek bed; handy because there were usually a few isolated pools of water along its length which cattle and sheep could drink from in the dry season, while on their way to somewhere else.

During the harrowing winter of 1862, an unusually wet winter I might add, a drover called

Mick McGurk was droving cattle through the area, heading for somewhere else, when he was halted by this creek - by this time a raging torrent of a creek. There was obviously no way that Mick was going to get his cattle across until the creek went down, so he decided to set up camp on higher ground and sit it out. Rumour has it that the spot he camped on is now the administrative block of the *Wudgi Sanatorium for the Criminally Insane*. An apt place to camp, one might think. Mick thought so!

Well, the long and the short of it is that the creek just never did go down, not in McGurk's lifetime, anyway, and he and the other drovers in the gang eventually got fed up with sitting around a camp-fire every night, roasting possums and tapping their feet to that insidious brand of country music as played by Jeremiah Warthog, drovers cook, on two coconuts and a tin whistle.

"For god's sake, Jeremiah, don't you know any other tunes? 'The Wild Colonial Boy' is a bit much after five hundred variations!" It was the clip-clopping of the coconuts that was driving them all to drink.

The boredom eventually became so intense that in one frantic ten day burst of activity, the three men - not counting Jeremiah of course - built a Pub.

After playing with names like "The Drover's Dog", and "The Travellers Arms", they gave it away for the evening, and sat around dreaming how fine it would be if their pub had beer, and a barmaid - especially a barmaid!

The next day Mick was down testing the banks of the creek, to see if there were any signs of them drying out.

"What's it like," yelled Jack Turnip, from a safe distance.

"It's a bit squidgy," Mick replied, tentatively. "No; not so much squidgy as... uh.... Wudgi!"

"Oh... Wudgi is it," Jack said, disappointed. He had hoped for something a little firmer. Still, Wudgi was better than Sludgy.

"I've got it! Wudgi - Wudgi Crossing! That's what we'll call it! What about "The Wudgi Arms" - for our Pub?"

As both these suggestions were taken up, it was Jack Turnip we can thank for giving our town such a memorable name, which is probably why the statue to him outside the old Wudgi stables has him sitting in a horse trough with a bucket on his head. But all this aside, Mick McGurk was of the opinion

9

that all the creek was good for was ducks - and in this he showed an incredible prescience - as if he *knew!* For in truth, that particular area has ever since been associated with ducks.

When civilisation finally came to the area in the shape of Pastor Gottenheim and his aunt Grendel, they built a little cottage just above the high water mark and kept ducks and geese. Once they had shuffled off this mortal coil, Alice Peckersnipe had done the same. She bought the cottage as a deceased estate, and took over the ducks which were happily running riot by this time, leaving the entire caboodle to her niece as a going concern. Then recently Mrs. Olivia Bentwhistle had moved into the place, and she had actually bred the ducks for market. She also sold live ducks to all and sundry, and made quite a nice thing out of it on the side.

But the curious thing was that on the other side of the creek lived a family called Ducks, and though they have been there for three generations or more - they never kept ducks at all.

The Ducks were rather better off than those residents on the other side of the creek, and consequently tended to give themselves airs. The current generation consisted of Selmore Ducks and his wife, Tenda. Selmore was a practising solicitor, and his wife a society hostess, if such a thing applied to Wudgi. They certainly had all the right contacts, though they were a strange couple to look at. He was all of 4' 11" tall, and she only 4' 8". This had prompted the local wits to coin the term "Ducks disease", which eventually leaked out to the world at large as those: "with their tail feathers too close to the ground."

There were two young children of the marriage; Apricot, who was a pretty little thing with pigtails, and Barton, who was a brain, and who was to eventually top the State in his bar exams. They say that it was Barton who was responsible for the saying - "Dux of the Course". But that was later.

Living right next door, in a 47 room retirement cottage consisting of three stories and a Norman Keep, was Sir Humphrey Aberfoyle Stubbit, a retired Judge of the Supreme Court of New South Wales. Although now 87 years of age, his vast experience was sometimes brought to bear in his capacity as a local magistrate in the little court at Wudgi. He was a great friend of the Ducks, and had done no small amount in the furtherance of Selmore's career. Thus it was that when two unlikely incidents occurred in juxtaposition, or so

11

it seemed, Magistrate Stubbit was on the bench to hear at least one of them. The resulting scandal proved to be a horrific climax to an inept career.

Constable Larry Gormenghastly was newly arrived from the city at that time, and had not yet adjusted to country ways, otherwise the following might never have happened. But in his zeal for recognition by his superiors, and in his hurry to get back to a civilised posting - meaning one near the 'Jug and Anchor' at Hindmarsh - he tended to be a little over-eager in his methods. In the short time since he had arrived in Wudgi he had managed to book four people for jay-walking across the main street, one of whom was old Elias Carbunkle in his wheelchair.

The good country people of Wudgi thought that Constable Gormenghastly would be laughed out of court, but to their dismay Sir Humphrey Stubbit was on the bench, and he was a stickler for a law-abiding population. He fined them all forty dollars, and added a rider in Elias's case that his wheelchair was to be clamped for 24 hours.

Wudgi folk were outraged. There wasn't a set of traffic lights within a hundred kilometers of Wudgi, and the only danger to pedestrians was Mrs Delaney, riding her three-wheeler up the footpath and into the general store. There was a muttering for some days, then the wiser of the community said: "Don't worry about Gormenghastly, give him enough rope..." And that was that.

The good Constable did not restrict his predatory behaviour to daylight hours, but had a tendency to stalk the night. His natty new police car could often be seen tailing women pushing prams, or hidden behind hedges waiting for the hippie community to appear smoking maridge-juana, as he insisted on calling it. Occasionally there was a real car he could tail, bouncing gingerly along the dirt road, and anything moving at over 30kph rarely failed to be pulled over. If he couldn't think of anything else, it was a licence check. If his victim was a long-hair, a drug search!

One dark night Mrs. Olivia Bentwhistle was driving suspiciously out of town at 11p.m., when the Constable's car just happened to appear behind her. She had been busy all day, and was just delivering some ducks to an old friend at Addlebury. It was the only chance she was going to get for a couple of days, as she had a heavy schedule in front of her. When she heard the siren, and saw the flashing blue light in her rear vision mirror, she breathed a sigh of annoyance and pulled over.

"Just a routine check, Madam," said the Constable, officiously. "Would you mind getting out of the car?"

Olivia Bentwhistle obliged. She realised that it was quicker to cooperate and get it over and done with, than to try to argue.

"Licence please," said Gormenghastly. Olivia handed over her licence, and shuffled impatiently from one foot to the other.

"O-ho - something not right here", thought the good Constable. "She's fidgety, guilty about something by the look of it."

He took out his torch and inspected the inside of the car, front and back.

"Look, Constable, I'm really in a hurry. It's late, and I'd like to get back home before midnight, if that's possible."

The Constable nodded.

"Check your boot!" he snapped.

Olivia opened the boot, and as the Constables torch lit up the interior, four little sets of eyes shone unblinkingly back at him.

"What's this then?"

"Ducks! What does it look like? I'm delivering them to a customer."

"A likely story," breathed the Constable, now hot on the trail of what was shaping up to be some sort of nefarious deed. He was determined to get to the bottom of it.

Lying in the boot in a neat little row were four ducks, each on its back, their legs tied together, another ligature around each body to keep the wings from flapping.

"I think you'd better come along with me, Madam. We can sort this out at the station."

Mrs. Bentwhistle's protests were in vain. He drove triumphantly behind her to the station, and once inside locked her up in the only cell for the night.

The previous week Sir Humphrey Stubbit had been perturbed to discover that his friends, the Ducks, had apparently left town without informing anyone. He was rather annoyed about it, because that morning he had discovered three families, four pigs and a dog had been squatting, unobserved, in the west wing of his cottage for the last three and a half years. They had claimed squatters' rights, and he wanted to engage Selmore to act for him in the matter.

Unbeknownst to him, the Ducks were soaking up the sun on Queensland's Gold Coast, after having won an all expenses paid trip for collecting 32,000 Green Tea Coupons over a fourteen-year period. The competition had actually lapsed ten years before, but the sponsors decided that such single mindedness should be rewarded. It was all very sudden and unexpected, so the family had left without informing anyone.

In the dock the following morning, Mrs. Bentwhistle was looking none too happy after a rough night on an old army blanket. Magistrate Stubbit was ushered in -"All rise" - and then they all settled in for an interesting session.

"First case - Ducknapping," said the clerk.

"What was that? Ducknapping?" Stubbit was suddenly as alive to the proceedings as 87 years will allow.

Constable Gormenghastly stepped forward to give his evidence.

"At approximately 11p.m. on the night of 11th. November, 1999, I was routinely patrolling the streets of Wudgi, when ..."

"Yes yes, do go on," said Stubbit, impatiently. "Skip all that. Let's get to the heart of the matter."

"Well, after doing routine checks of Mrs. Bentwhistle's car, I asked her to open the boot, and there..." - he paused for effect.

"Yes man, do get on with it..."

"I found the ducks!"

"You found the Ducks!" Stubbit's eyebrows shot up like a pair of arrowheads, and buried themselves in his scalp.

"Yes sir, all four of them, tied up in the back. Mrs. Bentwhistle had tied all their feet together, and had another loop around their middles. They were fairly well trussed, you may say!"

Sir Humphrey Stubbit appeared to be having an apoplectic fit. Finally he spoke:

"Dastardly! Trussed, you say. Dastardly! So that's where they got to..." The Judge cupped his mouth and said in a lowered aside to the clerk: "I had been expecting them for dinner on Wednesday. No wonder they didn't arrive."

Mrs Bentwhistle looked perplexed, and made to speak, but was waved to silence by the clerk.

"Now Constable Gormenghastly, how were the Ducks when you found them - not - er - dead, I hope."

"No your honour. I can relieve you on that point. Their little eyes kept blinking at me from under the boot lid."

"I would ask you to avoid referring to, er, physical size in your evidence Constable. The

17

word 'little' is unnecessary. We all know what you mean."

He turned to Mrs Bentwhistle.

"And you, Madam. Here you are, a comely woman in the prime of life! What on earth possessed you? This is very serious, very serious indeed. In all my years on the bench, never have I heard such a tale. You should be ashamed of yourself. What could you possibly be hoping to gain from such an act?"

"Oh, about thirty..." Olivia Bentwhistle began, but was shouted down by the judge.

"Of course, of course - Ransom!" Sir Humphrey exploded. "Not a huge amount, as these things go these days, but thirty 'big ones' would no doubt keep you in clover for a while, eh, Madam. And what then, when the money's spent, what then? I suppose you'd have done it again!"

"Of course - it's my living," said Mrs Bentwhistle, aggrieved.

"Shameless! You shameless hussy! Do you know the penalty of the law for this kind of thing? - Hanging, Madam, hanging!"

The clerk interposed at this juncture with a whispered aside to the magistrate.

"Oh, don't they? Well more's the pity then.

Well, life imprisonment – twenty-five years at the very least. TWENTY FIVE YEARS, MADAM!!!!"

He was speaking to no-one, however, for Olivia Bentwhistle had fainted in the dock at the word - 'hanging!'

"Get her on her feet," commanded Stubbit, and Olivia was dosed with salts and groggily returned to the land of the living.

"What were you going to do with... er ..." he looked down and consulted his notes, "Selmore?" Stubbit asked.

"Sell more? Yes, I'd sell more if I could. It's not against the law is it?"

"Against the law," boomed Stubbit. "Where have you *been* all your life, woman? Oh, I get it. Is this the insanity plea?" He looked at the clerk; the clerk shrugged his shoulders.

"I suppose you're going to say you weren't responsible for your actions, you did it in your sleep, the devil made you do it, you had a bad childhood, you fell in with the wrong crowd, you had a bad hair day..."

"No, not at all," said Olivia, puzzled.

"What was it then, a mental aberration, a moment of madness, a sudden urge, an irresistible impulse... drugs?"

"Certainly not," said Olivia, angrily.

"Silence, Madam! When I want you to speak I shall say so! Selmore indeed! And Tenda... Tenda, hey?"

"All the ducks are tender, I stake my reputation on it. They cook up a treat!"

There was a stunned silence.

"Heaven forbid," shouted the honourable Stubbit, throwing his hands in the air. "You *monster!*" he roared.

"Cannibalism! You've hit on a ring of perverts, Gormenghastly. You must question this woman, get the names of her associates, break this gourmet ring once and for all."

Gormenghastly was looking rather uncomfortable by this time.

"And how are they served up, Madam, if I may be so bold as to ask," said Sir Humphrey, sarcastically, leaning gloweringly over the bench.

"With an apricot sauce, how else," replied Mrs. Bentwhistle, totally confused by now at what all the fuss was about.

"APRICOT - Apricot - dear sweet little Apricot; you would do that - SAUCE*!!!*"

Mrs. Bentwhistle could contain herself no

longer.

"What's wrong with apricot duck? Are you a vegetarian or something?"

Sir Humphrey Stubbit's eyes almost bugged out.

"Frivolity! In my courtroom!"

In a moment of judicial lunacy, Olivia Bentwhistle was sentenced to fifty years hard labour, to be flogged three times a year through the streets of Wudgi, to have her eyes put out with red-hot pokers and to be stretched on the rack. And as he considered the sentence to be such a lenient one, she would get no time off for good behaviour.

Sir Humphrey Aberfoyle Stubbit was a broken man that day as he left the bench. Mrs Bentwhistle had collapsed yet again, and was being carried out in handcuffs when the clerk of the court thought to introduce to the magistrate, after the hearing, the principals of the case - the four ducks.

They say that Sir Humphrey's rooms are more than comfortable in the Wudgi Sanatorium for the Criminally Insane. He eats heartily and well, but for some reason will not countenance duck on the menu.

Mrs Bentwhistle decided to try a less dangerous occupation - cleaning! She scrubs out the rooms of the W.S.C.I., and occasionally tips a bucket of hot soapy water over Sir Humphrey's feet, whenever there's nobody else around.

Harry's Homecoming

Harry Hardcastle gazed pensively through the windscreen of his car. It had been a long drive, nearly two thousand kilometres, but it was almost over now. The sun shone brilliantly on the pebble lenses of his thick spectacles, and he debated whether or not to pull over until the sun settled down on the other side of the hill.

There was a slight thump under the car, and he looked in the mirror to note the flattened form of a sleepy lizard in his wake, that he had blindly annihilated due to the sun blazing in his eyes. With a tut of annoyance he slowed down and pulled off the road.

He mentally added the sleepy to the seventeen furry, scaly, feathered and other pancake shaped mammals that he had despatched over a seventeen-hundred-kilometre stretch, and figured that it could have been worse.

It was his sight, of course. He always blamed that! The wonder was that he had a licence to drive at all. Once behind the wheel of a car, at a distance of over twenty meters, Harry couldn't see a thing. There was just this blurred distance that he drove at, only taking evasive action if something in that radius moved unexpectedly, or turned from green to red.

But Harry had gritted his teeth and clung grimly to the steering wheel. Nothing would stop him now his mind was made up. Harry was going *home!*

It had been thirteen years since he had last been in this part of the country, and if it wasn't for his mother, he wouldn't be here now. She was declining, poor thing, and his father had suffered a stroke, and relapsed into silence.

Not that he had ever been very talkative - Harry's mother had seen to that. Getting a word in edgeways with Harry's mother had been almost impossible when he was growing up, and Harry could remember his father valiantly trying to speak for half an hour once, while his mother carried on a tirade about how 'careless the lot of them were, and how she had to think of everything, and no-one did anything around the house and she had to pick up and clean and wash and *what thanks did she ever get* - None, and that's a fact; and why she ever left a comfortable home in the city to marry a ne'er do well like her husband and settle in a black hole like Wudgi Crossing, well, *she should have had her head read;* and as for the kid - (the kid was Harry's other name when he was growing up) -

well it must have been genital because it certainly didn't come from her side of the family because she had brothers that had become lawyers and Eldermen or something, councillors anyway, with very important folio's and she had been quite a beauty in her day and very much in demand at the local dances and could have had her *pick* of any number of young men but no; her father had pushed her at William (Harry's Dad) because he *thought* William was a *pastoralist* with a million sheep or something and a lot of *verdant pastures* whatever they were, not the lousy stinking bog of forty seven acres a goat two pigs and a dried up milk cow that William had the effrontery to call a farm for god's sake and that she hadn't found out about until she got there on her wedding day only to fall flat on her face in a cow clap and it's never got any better from that day to this and she *wouldn't have minded* if there was some gratitude to be had for all the years of sacrifice but for all she could see there wasn't and if brains were bullets there wouldn't be enough between Harry and the old man together to put a decent end to it all; but they *shouldn't think* that just because she hadn't left up to that point that she wouldn't because there's *a time and a place for everything* and just maybe that time was coming up like an express train and they might just have to muck out for themselves in future because she'd *come to the end of her rope,'* - and so it had gone on for another dreary fifteen minutes.

Harry sat at the side of the road, and smiled. When she'd finally run out of breath, the old man said, quietly:

"The chicken's been on fire for the last ten minutes!"

Sure enough, black smoke was pouring out of the oven door and flames were engulfing the remains of the evening meal. That was the best meal Harry never got. It was worth it just to see his mother's face. As far as he remembered, though, it had all worked out all right, because his dad patted his mother on the backside and carted her off to bed, and everything was sweet as roses the following day. So maybe the old man didn't talk much, but he must have had something to tame the raging beast in his mother.

Harry had never married. He felt as if he'd lived through half a dozen marriages before he turned eighteen, and though his Dad would have liked to see him settle at home on the scrubby farm, Harry knew that he had to leave and put enough miles between himself and home to ensure that the black thoughts he'd been having for some years would be allowed to sink back into his subconscious mind and, perhaps, with peace and quiet, eventually leave him forever.

As a youth he had often passed the gates of the Wudgi Sanatorium for the Criminally Insane, and there was always this sneaking suspicion in the back of his mind that those gates were just waiting to open up for him.

What gave him this idea were the convulsive movements he would sometimes make, quite involuntarily, with the potato peeler, or the lemon juicer at those times when his mother's mouth was vibrating at a hundred miles an hour in his direction. Indeed, once, one of his more demonstrative lunges almost took off his mother's ear, before he came back to his senses and realised what he was doing.

No, he'd had to get away, and for the first ten years he'd managed to escape with only a bare visit home about once every two and a half years. But after the fourth visit, he left for thirteen years, and had never gone back - until now. Twenty-three years since leaving home, he thought with satisfaction, and not a regret.

Or was there? She was his mother, after all, and Harry was not so totally cut off that he didn't feel anything. It had been a pity about his father. Largely recovered from the stroke, he was looking after himself all right, but had been left with a serious speech impediment - fated perhaps, after a lifetime of not being able to speak when he needed to.

But his mother! She was in the Wudgi Crossing Nursing Home, suffering from alzheimers, and blissfully unaware of who she was or who William was when he came to visit. No doubt the same would apply to Harry. She'd hardly remember him after thirteen years.

While Harry was busily musing about his past on the side of the road, a passing snake felt itself magnetically attracted to the heat of his engine, and slithering under the car managed to rise up and wrap itself comfortably around the air cleaner.

Starting the car once more, Harry narrowly avoided remodelling the side of a speeding sedan that swept past him as he pulled blindly back onto the road. Only ten kilometres, and he'd be there. He thought that he'd better go home first and see his father, then in the morning he would go and see his mother and try to make amends in some way for being so inaccessible over all these years.

William answered the door after a few minutes of shuffling about inside, and stared at his son as if trying to recall where he'd seen that face before.

"It's me, Dad - Harry."

A gleam of recognition entered the old man's eye, and he stood aside to allow the visitor access. Once seated in the comfortable lounge room, Harry cast his eye about approvingly. Not a lot had changed. There was some new furniture, and some he remembered from when he was a lad.

"How have you been getting on, Dad," Harry shouted, mistaking his father's condition as being one that incorporated deafness.

William made a couple of attempts to reply, then mumbled something like *"Mustard Gumble!"*

"I see," nodded Harry, rather at a loss for a reply.

"You look as if you're managing okay," said Harry after a couple of minutes.

"Iss vair corple under rear - naw; nar corple, quillept," replied his father, correcting himself. "Quollop - kitel - Kywet - Kw..."

"Quiet -you mean quiet! It's very quiet around here; is that what you mean," said Harry, with a sudden blaze of understanding. William nodded his head vigorously, beaming at Harry like a child. It was the first time that anyone had understood a word he'd said for the past six months.

After that there was no stopping him.

"Saw martyr gong toddy an tooder, bud mummer nod knewed-yod com." William sucked on his pipe in satisfaction.

After twenty minutes of close questioning Harry gleaned that the meaning ran something like; 'saw your mother today, but her memory's gone, told her you were coming but she couldn't remember you."

They spent the rest of the evening smiling at each other, and occasionally breaking out into telepathic chortles.

The next morning Harry left his father swilling out the three pigs, and drove around to the Nursing Home. It was a very old establishment, and very dark inside, but he eventually managed to stumble across what appeared to be a nursing sister. After explaining what he was there for, he was directed to room 37, and left to his own devices.

"You don't mind if I take her out for a drive," Harry called after her departing figure.

"Not at all Mr. Hardcastle, just have her back for tea at five."

There didn't appear to be a room 37. There was a 36 and a 38, but 37 certainly wasn't in the area unless it was that foul looking broom closet that he stumbled into, in which an old lady was laying about her with a mop, and giving the wash-stand a severe drubbing.

Harry staggered back, said "Sorry!" and left the old lady to it. She had glared at him in an un-nerving way, debating whether or not to take the broom to the intruder or just complete the demolition of her husband's new chook pens.

There was no recognition from either party, so Mrs. Hardcastle kept swinging, and Harry wandered off.

Further up the passage he pushed open the door of 36, and saw an old lady, seated in a wheelchair, with her back to him at the window.

Mrs. Featherspoon had been watching him staggering short-sightedly along the narrow path for the last five minutes, and wondered who the blithering idiot was who had let a lunatic loose in the grounds. She had lost her power of speech, but not of thought, and though she was wheelchair bound she wasn't a total invalid.

But it suited her to be pushed around in her chair, and she felt it only her due after raising a family of six who had all buggered off the moment she had her first stroke. She had been fond of barking at her brood - as they were growing up - "when you grow up you can look after me in my old age; that's what I had you for, and that's what you'll do."

They'd all left home at fifteen, leaving her with no-one to grumble at, or to hit on the head with her collection of saucepans. Now she was stuck in this nursing home, so she was going to make the best of it.

The only time she got out of her chair unaided was when none of the staff were around. But while they were, she always had the bell to summons them, and summons them she did - ten times a day!

Suddenly there was a movement behind her, and she turned her head with a start. Before she knew it a pair of wet lips had attached themselves to her forehead, and appeared to be attempting to suck her brain out through her cranium.

"Hi Mum, it's only me - Harry. Let me look at you."

The wheelchair suddenly spun around 180 degrees, and Mrs. Featherspoon found herself looking into the myopic eyes of the lunatic from the garden path.

"Gee, you have changed," muttered Harry, taken aback. "I knew you hadn't been well, but I didn't realise what this old timers disease could do to you. Haven't your eyebrows got hairy?"

Mrs. Featherspoon felt her mouth drop open, but no sound would issue forth.

"See, you're surprised to see me! I knew you would be," said Harry, making allowances for this woman who suddenly had a nose twice as big as the one he could remember on his mother.

"We're just going to have to get re-acquainted, you and I" said Harry. "I've come to take you for a drive in the country," he added, thinking that he'd better explain to her what he was doing.

It was worse than he thought. Not only had this dreadful illness and the intervening years changed his mother beyond recognition, but with her mouth hanging open like that she looked like an idiot. Perhaps that's what happened in the end! The journey through life was merely a passage between infancy and idiocy...

Spinning the chair around, Harry pushed off down the corridor at a brisk pace, with Mrs. Featherspoon frantically hanging onto the rubber tyres to prevent herself from being kidnapped. But she was no match for Harry's strength. By the time they got to the door Harry noticed tell-tale wisps of blue smoke pouring off her fingertips, and he thoughtfully stopped long enough to pry her fingers loose from the tyres and drop them, still smouldering, into her lap.

"Ooyer, alp-alp, leggorov me," Mrs. Featherspoon finally managed to squeeze out.

"Don't worry Mum, going for a drive is quite painless. We'll have a chat!"

Mrs. Featherspoon's slippers were clamped so solidly to the vinyl floor during this race along the passage that her soles became red hot, and she began to fling her feet about in gay abandon, uttering gurgling noises that Harry took for words of appreciation.

"That's okay, Mum, you don't have to thank me. We'll have a great day. I'll take you over to see Dad."

Harry might have been myopic, but he was strong, and soon had the struggling Mrs. Featherspoon in the passenger seat of his car.

"Yulp - yullup!" she cried. "Alp-alp!" But Harry was doing a treat at this translation stuff by now, and replied:

"Yup! That's right -Yup." Then he burst into a stanza of *'We're off to see the Wizard, the wonderful Wizard of Oz,'* as they sped off.

Mrs. Featherspoon sat in a dread panic; he must be a looney - she'd have to humour him. How the hell did you humour someone when you couldn't speak?

Harry stopped a few times along the winding country roads to let his 'mother' make the most of the scenery. A large brown cow came nuzzling up to the passenger window, and Mrs. Featherspoon let out an involuntary "yallup" before she realised that the cow was an idiot, too. She played with the idea of dropping a note:

"Kidnapped - Save me from this looney."

 but then realised that she didn't know where they were going, didn't have a pencil or paper, and couldn't write the blasted thing anyway.

At his father's gate, Harry slowed down.

"Now you remember this place, don't you Mum? You couldn't forget this place!"

Out of the shrubbery rose a shadowy figure, old William, covered in pig effluent, mud, and giving off an odour somewhat akin to goat's breath.

Harry pulled up by the house and got out to walk around to the passenger door. He stopped to chat to his father for a few moments, who appeared to be having some sort of a fit as he stared pop-eyed at the woman in the car.

"Gawd; ain't she changed," he muttered to himself.

It was fortuitous that at that moment, the snake, finding it rather hot under the bonnet, managed to discover a hole in the firewall especially provided for the clutch, and flattening itself out slid quietly and unobtrusively - or so it thought - into the relative cool of the car. Mrs. Featherspoon felt something brush against her leg, and looked down.

As Harry opened the door there was a high pitched "whoop", and a fat old crippled lady suddenly bounded out of her seat, ran up Harry's chest and left him gasping on the ground as she dashed into the house, 'alping' for all she was worth. Old William suddenly grinned, and followed in her general direction as the snake made its getaway out through the open door. Harry, flat on his back, didn't even see it.

In the house William was patting Mrs Featherspoon on the back, and trying to tone down the whoops as she got her breath back. He couldn't get over how much his wife had come along since that stay in the nursing home. Edie had never been able to gallop like that before. By the time Harry got to the door, the old man was remembering feelings that he hadn't had for forty years.

Harry decided to leave them to it.

"See you later, folks," he called out. "I'm off to the pub. See you in an hour or so!"

Back at the nursing home Mrs. Hardcastle was being forcibly separated from her mop, and returned to her room on the other side of the nursing home.

"I thought he was taking her out," the sister was saying. "He said he was her son! Just goes to show - you can't trust anyone these days."

The Guided Tour

It was the annual meeting of the Wudgi Progress Association, and there were a lot of glum faces in the Old Hall that night because news had just come through that Wudgi's great rivals in the tourism stakes had scored a coup. Addlebury was to get a Motel.

"It seems they've stolen it, right from under our noses," wailed Mrs. Harkpea, the P.A.'s long-suffering secretary. "If only Col Springett had sprayed his bottom, and got rid of those damned mosquito's, I'm sure the developers would have come here."

"His bottom paddock you mean," said Angus McSoufflé, a stickler for rectitude.

"How many rooms," said Mrs. Blithe-Brown.

"Twelve I believe," said the vicar, who was the current Treasurer of the Association's seventy-two dollars and sixty cents - mainly because he was the only one in the community that couldn't afford to leave town.

Mrs. Blithe-Brown sniffed, in that rather superior way of hers, and intoned: "only *twelve* rooms, oh dear me; I don't know that we've missed out on that much."

"Well it's more than we've got in Wudgi, Maude," said our illustrious President, Jim Mopandle. "Let's face it, tourism is the *'in thing'* these days, and what have we got to offer the average tourist? We haven't even got a Motel for them to stay in!"

"But we've got the Wudgi Arms Hotel. Surely there's enough accommodation there, Jim," said Bill Beakheaper."

"If you don't mind sleeping on a chaff bag, next to a barrel of rough Red," sniffed Mrs. Blithe-Brown, who'd suffered a humiliating personal experience there when she was young. There was a sudden silence here, as *"Rough"* Red happened to be the nickname of the Mayor.

It was all gloom for another twenty minutes while a desultory conversation was carried on regarding Wudgi's tourist attractions. At the end of it, it had to be admitted that these consisted of Mrs. O'Malley's vegetable garden, which had somehow spread out onto the footpath so that pedestrians had to walk in the road to avoid trampling her zucchini's, and Merv Malachi's twisted chimney, which for the past twenty years had looked perilously close to toppling from his cottage into the street, and flattening the first tourist to come into sight.

Suddenly there was an excited exclamation from Wally Witherspoon, who usually slept through these meetings, and whom everyone thus thought was having a nightmare.

"Oh-wo-uhh! Hang on! What about the cemetery?" exclaimed Wal. "Now that's a real tourist attraction in itself - and Addlebury hasn't got one to hold a candle to ours. We could have a guided tour!"

"A guided tour?" sniffed Mrs. Blithe-Brown, "of the Cemetery?"

Her very tone was calculated to convince Wally that he had suddenly gone raving mad, and that perhaps he'd better shut up before he landed in the Wudgi Sanatorium for the Criminally Insane. But Wal would not be moved, and in a way his idea was not half bad. There were so many strange characters lying in that cemetery that a guided tour could be good for tourism, and bring both visitors and their wallets into the town.

After all, there was Zacariah Cribb, the town's funeral director, who had actually died at the burial of his childhood sweetheart, and had dropped onto her coffin causing no end of a fuss. Then there was the Malone family, brought to grief by their preoccupation with the state of their toilet pan. There was *'Desperate Dan'* DeVilliers, an extremely early settler in the region who had decided, in the 1870's, to pack up and go fortune hunting in America. After a bar-room brawl in San Francisco, which ended up in a shoot-out, DeVilliers found himself sentenced to the Electric Chair.

Back in Wudgi, his estranged wife told their nine-year old daughter that they were "giving your father the electric chair today."

Young Ellen DeVilliers thought this was marvellous, and told all her friends at school that her father was being honoured in the United States; they were presenting him with a new-fangled chair. When his body was finally extradited by the family, back to Australia, Ellen went looking for the chair and was disgusted that they hadn't forwarded this on as well.

So many characters; so many stories!

What about Albert Pennypicker, the water-cart man, who had been so stingy during the long drought of 1889 that an old lady had almost died of thirst because she didn't have the sixpence to pay him for a jug of water. The footnote to that was quite interesting, because like all miserable people,

Albert Pennypicker got his in the end.

It seems that, being in the business so to speak, Albert had been determined that *he* was never going to run out of water. So he had an underground tank put in beneath his kitchen, so that he could 'sit' on his valuable water supply every night. Well, one night a neighbour came to chide him about his miserliness with the water cart, and Albert had sat calmly at his dinner table, ignoring the repeated attacks made upon his character.

"Pass the water jug my dear," he said to his wife, as he washed down an extra large slice of apple pie. At this the visitor turned prodigiously nasty, and invoked the ancient gods. He wagged his forefinger at the sinner and swore on Neptune's scaly head that Albert would meet with a bitter end.

Suddenly the old wooden floor gave out a horrendous creak and Albert and his brood all disappeared into the water tank, along with the floor, kitchen table, chairs, and apple pie.

The visitor stood in the doorway, puzzled, and then stared in horror at his potent forefinger. Later that day he went home and chopped it off with an axe in case he wagged it, by mistake, at anyone else. Septicaemia set in, and he was dead within the week.

Most of the locals shook their heads, and thought he had over-reacted a bit to the deaths of the Pennypicker family. But Lorenzo Hellfinger had always been a little superstitious about his name, and this, he thought, proved it!

The Pennypicker and Hellfinger graves are all in a line at row 5, aisle 12.

Fred Feeble, our local storekeeper cleared his throat, and addressed the meeting.

"Well I'm against it. I don't think that something so undignified as a guided tour through the cemetery could bring us anything but ridicule."

We all nodded sympathetically, and then were silent for a long time. It was an embarrassed silence, because *we all knew* why Fred was against it, and *he knew we knew;* which was why he got up to leave shortly after that, and we all looked knowingly at each other.

"Bob the Bodgie," remarked President Jim, and we all nodded again.

Bob the Bodgie! *That* was a name to conjure with! It had all happened in the late '50's, when Wudgi was even more out of the way than it is today, and city visitors were few and far between.

It must have been 1957 when Rock 'n' Roll suddenly appeared in Wudgi in the guise of a bodgie and his widgie. (In actual fact, the two were merely transposed Teddy Boy and Teddy Girl, as they had arrived from Cockney London as immigrants only months before).

However; one day there was a thunderous roar up the main street, and to those who were around, (which was precious few at that time of day), appeared a vision of hell. Sitting astride a Triumph Thunderbird, and draped in black leather, hair slicked back with a whole jar of Brylcreem, was a mother's worst nightmare. His name was Bob, it appeared, and he represented the new breed of Rockers 'n' Rollers from the city of iniquity. But worse, seated behind him on the pillion seat was what a Wudgi-ite would at best have called a fast little hussy, and at worst - a tart. This girl had orange and green hair; obviously a Catholic *and* a Protestant - if that were possible; and her clothes aped the clothes of the fellow she was with. Skin tight jeans - ("they left nothing to the imagination, Cora, *Nothing...")* - *a* frilly, lace-trimmed blouse, and to top it off, a leather jacket two sizes too big. They alighted from the motorbike, stretched like a couple of Neanderthals, then swaggered along the main street. (Swaggered may not be quite the word I'm looking for here, because their gait was far more intimidating than that. It said - "We're looking for Trouble" - with a capital 'T').

Fred Feeble's father was in charge of the store in those days, Amos; and old Amos Feeble was known to be a bit nervous and unstable even then. In fact some went as far as to say that he was humourless, a bit thick - that he was to sanity what a currant is to a Christmas pudding. As it turned out, they were right.

Now old Amos had lived a real country life, a sheltered life you might say, and he'd certainly avoided the city like the plague. So he wasn't exactly *au fait* with what passed as normal in the metropolis in those heady days, and when these two denizens of the new youth approached his shop, who is to say what went on in his mind?

Inside the doorway of the shop was a birdcage, one of those painted wire ones hanging from a frame, and in this cage was a budgie. The bird was Amos's pet, his pride and joy, and he fed it little titbits throughout the day; fed it so often in fact that this little budgie had grown to be quite round and fat.

When Bob and Wyn, (that was the Widgie's

name), walked in, they were immediately drawn to the bird.

"'Ere, Wyn, look a' this. What sort'a bird is this then? In't it big."

"Sa Canary I fink", said the tart, and Amos glowered at them from behind his counter. Canary indeed!

"Budgie", he said, sharply, not to mince words.

"Budgie ... ? *Budgie* ... ?" said Bob, menacingly. "For your information it's "Bodgie", an' I'll 'ave yer know, we're prahd of it!"

"Bodgie?" said Amos, startled. *"Bodgie?* Where do you come from? Round here it's pronounced 'Budgie', and I'll ask you to keep your hands off it."

Bob looked at Wyn.

"Is 'e insulting me? He keeps callin' me a budgie." He turned menacingly to Amos and leant over the counter.

"Listen you ole git, you call me a budgie one more time an' I'll take that canary of yours an' wring its neck. Where the bloody 'ell are we anyway. What is this place - the town that god forgot or somefink'?"

Amos started going purple in the face. Wring his bird's neck? Despite himself, he suddenly

46

heard his voice answering the question:

"Wudgi", he snapped, and by the look he got in return from this young thug, he knew he'd said the wrong thing.

"Wudgi? Bloody Wudgi? Do you hear what he's callin' *you*, doll? Wudgi! I'm gonna do the bleeder..."

Turning to the shopkeeper he screamed

"Widgie ... Widgie... do you get it? Call my bird a Wudgi again and it'll be a bunch of fives for you, mate!"

"It's not your bird, it's my bird," Amos yelled in exasperation, and something approaching panic.

Bob's eyes began to bug out, and Wyn took hold of his arm to hold him back.

"Don't do nuffin' stoopid, Bob," she warned. "E's not worf it!"

"Not worf it," yelled Bob. "First 'e calls you a Wudgi, then 'e says you're *his* bird, not *mine!*"

He turned to the cage, wrenched open the door and in a sudden movement grabbed hold of the fat little bird. Then he waved the captive in Amos's face.

"I've a good mind to squawk this one right now!"

Amos panicked. "Don't hurt him. I've had him

for years - he talks to me..."

"Well he's fat, big 'n fat; who ever saw a big fat canary before."

"A big fat Budgie," Amos corrected, and watched Bob's face go a mottled sort of colour.

"You callin' me a fat budgie you old twit? God, Wyn... fat; 'e's callin' me fat!"

Amos really panicked now.

"No, not you! I wasn't calling you fat - just the bird!"

Wyn exploded.

"Why you *ole barsket!* Right, that's it then - I won't stop you this time, Bob, *let 'im ave it!"*

Bob tightened his grip on the budgie, and shook it in Amos's face.

"You've insulted the Widgie, mate. Yer might get away with it wiv me, but not wiv 'er."

"I've lived here all my life," said Amos, shaking uncontrollably. "It's *always* been Wudgi, and the budgie's *always* been a budgie - his name's Bob; *Bob the Budgie.* Have you got some sort of speech defect or something?"

"BOB THE BUDGIE," Bob exploded, "I keep telling you that it's Bob the Bodgie an' Wyn the Widgie, an' if you can't live with that, then I don't know where you're livin', mate!"

"WUDGI! WUDGI! - I should know, I've lived in Wudgi with Bob the Budgie for years," Amos yelled back.

"Right, that's it cobber! Your Bird's dead," said the bodgie, and with a quick flick of his wrist, Bob wrung its little neck.

Amos staggered back behind the counter in shock, and seemed to find it hard to breathe.

"I'll get you for that, you thug!"

"Oh yus, you an' who's army," sneered Bob, smugly.

"Get out, get out of my shop," Amos snarled at him, and Bob threw the remains of Bob the Budgie on the counter, in a flurry of little feathers.

"The next time you meet a Bodgie 'n Widgie, maybe you'll be a little nicer to 'em," sneered Bob, as the two renegades turned and left the shop.

Amos looked down at his dead Budgie, and his eyes glazed over. In a moment of grief and madness he dashed over to a tall cupboard and pulled out a mean looking double-barrelled shotgun. By the time the terrible two had done a victory tour of the main street and were heading back, Amos was ready for them. As they roared back towards his shop, Amos dashed out and pointed both barrels at the tank of the Trumpy

Thunderbird.

Before you could say *'Flaming Bombadiers'*, (even if for some reason you had wanted to), there were bits of Bodgie and Widgie floating down all over Wudgi.

It was all very sad of course, and could have been avoided if Amos had been more a man of the world. But he got very nice lodgings in the Wudgi Sanatorium for the Criminally Insane, and they let him out after seven years. He was never the same, of course, and went into solitary retirement.

Down on row 17, aisle 3, at the Wudgi Cemetery there is a plain stone in memory of Bob, and in row 18, aisle 4 there's another one for Wyn. There's a rumour around town that these were paid for by Amos, in atonement for his guilt, but I don't think that's strictly true. If he did arrange the headstones, he did it for entirely another reason.

You see, Bob's headstone bears the simple inscription; "In Memory of Bob, the Budgie"; and across the way another stone bears the statement, in a flowery script - "The Widgie of Wudgi."

A Question of Anastasia

Samuel Griptite stood uncomfortably in the corner of the little chemist's shop, hopping from one foot to the other in an agony of indecision. He had been there all morning, waiting for the undivided attention of the chemist. So far he had not caught so much of a glimpse of him, which was not surprising as Horus Archibilus had been out since dawn playing an imaginary game of golf with an imaginary set of golf clubs.

If Samuel hadn't been so agitated that day he would have realised that it was the chemist's regular morning for golf, and he would have waited until the afternoon.

Instead, the girl behind the counter had glared at him suspiciously every five minutes, as he hovered about among the nasal sprays, the liniment and the medical supports, to such effect that he had felt constrained to buy something, to justify his presence. Consequently, he now stood burdened down with two carrier bags full of sufficient pharmaceuticals to stupefy and embalm the entire population of Wudgi.

Among other things he now possessed eleven different tubes of toothpaste, each one guaranteed to beat, scrape, dissolve or burn your teeth into submission, while actually turning them any colour between green and orange during the active phase. Then there were seven different mouth-washes, the purchase of which had convinced the girl behind the counter that Samuel either had gargantuan bad breath, or the plague running around on his tongue, and this latter had persuaded her to wrap a scarf around her mouth and nose while he remained in the shop so that she could avoid the ill effects of either.

She stood now glowering at him like a Mexican bandit, willing him to rack off so that she could take off this stupid scarf.

Samuel made a faint attempt to be seen to be agonising over the merits of various aspirin, and then stood sideways to the counter, hoping that his lean figure would merge with the shelves, and convince the girl to leave the counter, go out the back and read her Mills and Boon. But she wasn't fooled for one moment. Indeed, every five minutes she made a point of leaning over the counter as far as she could, staring at him with glowering precision, and enquiring with a monotonous regularity:

"Can I help you, Sir?" Each time she did, he

bought something else.

Samuel was at something of a disadvantage in these exchanges, as he suffered from a nervous disorder which made him a prey to solecisms - the uttering of a wrong word for the one he meant to say. Thus, for a tin of band-aids he had asked for a tube of bandages, and though the girl had looked puzzled over the 'tube', she had supplied him with enough bandages to wrap the Town Hall in. For a can of aerosol spray he had substituted 'anal conditioner', and had received a tube of rectinol almost thrown at him across the counter.

Miss Curdlemouth had decided at this point that the man was a veritable cesspit of disease, and slipped a pair of rubber gloves on to compliment the scarf.

Griptite shivered, as if someone had just walked over his grave. The girl must know something, otherwise why the scarf, why the rubber gloves? His condition must be more contagious than he thought. Perhaps the doctor had phoned the chemist shop after he had left that morning to warn that a human time bomb was heading their way, and to take all precautions. Whatever happened to doctor/patient confidentiality he wondered, somewhat aggrieved.

The interview with the doctor that morning had been quite sobering. After noticing a slight rash on his chest when he got up, Samuel had decided to give himself the once over to discover if there were any other symptoms he should draw to the doctor's attention.

At first there was nothing, and then he remembered the pins and needles in his fingers that he got every time he sat on his hands for more than twenty minutes at a time. There was the shortness of breath, the chest pains, and the way his legs buckled under him after jogging twenty-five kilometres every morning. Then there were the vague stomach cramps, especially noticeable after eating two main and three dessert courses, the burning sensation he experienced each time he ate curry, the nights he couldn't sleep, the mornings he couldn't wake up, the raging desire to do something with his life, and the lethargy that crept over him each time he asked himself - 'What'?

Oh, there was something wrong, all right. Possibly something terminal! He turned to Doctor Derwent Pater-Proby and, in a piteous voice said: "Am I going to die, Doctor?"

Pater-Proby turned his philosopher's eye on the patient, smiled grimly, and then half-turned away.

"Most assuredly, Griptite, most assuredly." He would have added that we were all going to die, sooner or later; that the only thing we had in common on this earth was that nobody got out alive. But he was interrupted by the sound of Samuel Griptite's pink bottom hitting the floor, and was thereafter so concerned with bringing the fainting man around that he lost the thread of his time-honoured speech.

Pater-Proby scratched out a script for a course of Valium, and hardly heard the revived man's next question.

"How long, doctor?"

"A couple of weeks should do it. Now just get down to the chemist and collect these little fellows. They should relax you enough to help you through it."

Griptite staggered out, his mind in a daze.

He wondered if the chemist would give him something, a fatal dose, something for a quick, clean end. It would all depend on whether or not the chemist believed in Euthanasia or not. Griptite determined to ask him.

Horus Archibilus was meanwhile gyrating along the main street in a swirl of technicolour donkeys. Every now and then he stopped to hit an imaginary golf ball into the grinning mouth of the giant walrus that had pursued him from the banks of the creek. It was floating on a purple eiderdown, and shaving with a manhole cover.

Horus was somewhat annoyed. Why the town council didn't do something about these animals from the creek he really didn't know. He would bring it up at the next meeting.

Not that it would do any good! He had complained once about the astrakhan mouseholes that littered the main street, but nothing had been done. He had fallen down one only three weeks ago, and found himself in the den of a giant condor, but had they listened? Trying to get any sense out of the council was like trying to beat an egg with a bassoon.

Horus Archibilus was what you'd call a practising chemist. He practised all the time, at night, in the back room, mixing up little potions and pick-me-ups from the staggering array of chemicals on his shelves, and then trying them out to see what the effect was.

"I'd never give my clients anything that I wouldn't try myself," he would say proudly - when he was capable of speech, that was.

A lot of the time he hung out with the multi-coloured denizens of some strange subterranean world that hid in the shadows of Wudgi Crossing, with openings to it hovering in the shadows of the Fish and Chip shop and the Union Bank. He had once seen a teller snapped up by a pink artichoke behind the counter, and had immediately cancelled his account. Horus now only dealt with the Credit Union. Their statements were easier to read, anyway, as they were printed on Lamingtons in a neat, formal script.

Samuel Griptite breathed a sigh of relief as Horus whirled through the door of his shop, spinning on his axis three times as he crashed into the condom stand. Then he stopped, and stared blankly at the apparition behind the counter.

"Have you come to rob me or examine me," Horus exclaimed to the masked vision in rubber gloves.

Miss Curdlemouth ripped off the scarf.

"It's me! And this man won't leave me alone. He keeps on..." suddenly she burst into tears. "He keeps on asking for Thalium and Oxy-Acetylene and Rectal Vapour, and things that I've never heard of - and I've been here five years," she sobbed. "And I think he's just making it up so he can hang around here and watch me," she wailed. "I think he's a dirty old pervert, and he's got bad breath - or I think he has; why else would he want five mouth washes and eleven tubes of toothpaste, and I think he's got something and I don't want to catch it so I'm going home, and if you need me I'll be back in the morning," she blabbed, as she ran out of the shop.

Horus turned to Samuel Griptite, and shrugged.

"Porcupines," he muttered glumly, and went behind the counter.

Seeing his chance, Griptite advanced on him, thinking to get it over before anyone else came in.

"Do you believe in Anastasia," he hissed, pulling Horus up with a jerk.

Horus looked at him in alarm. Who was this turkey? On the other side of his counter stood a bright green turkey with two carrier bags full of pharmaceuticals. It appeared to be mumbling something about the Russian Royal House.

"Not personally. I'm Scottish you know!"

Griptite seemed bemused. Perhaps the Presbyterians had a thing about it. Perhaps the Scottish equivalent of the pope, Hamish McHaggis, had sent out an encyclical?

"Is there a bull about it," asked Griptite,

anxiously.

"I sincerely hope not, I've only just got rid of the Walrus," replied Archibilus. "Give me your scrip, please. I want to see if I can still read."

Griptite gave up in despair. Would no-one help him terminate his useless existence!

Horus wandered out the back and shortly returned with some gaily-coloured pills in a brown paper bag. The instructions read: "Take the white pills four times a day, the black twice a day until finished."

It wasn't until later that Griptite discovered that there were neither white nor black pills in his bag, only 200 grams of licorice bullets that Horus had mislaid the month before. He popped them anyway, all together, and waited for something to happen. It did! Diarrhoea!

In a frenzy of fear by this time, Samuel Griptite wrote a final note to his washerwoman, and made his preparations. Then he headed for the creek.

I should interject at this point to state that the creek at Wudgi Crossing is not as it used to be. When Mick McGurk and Co. were stranded there in the 1860's, there was absolutely no way across that raging torrent. He would have been most pleasurably surprised today, therefore, to note the handsome bridge that spans the creek, its red brick arch assuring travellers that never again would they be forced to spend another demented night at Wudgi Crossing.

Though built in the 1920's, and no wider than the width of a medium car, the bridge was the town's lifeline to Addlebury, and was irreplaceable. It was to this bridge that Samuel Griptite now repaired.

Captain Emmanuel Belchfire, the town's Fire Chief, was to tell the ensuing story many times after this, over a mug of flaming lager.

"It was Esmerelda Ripperchest that raised the alarm," he said. "She had been playing 'windscreen wipers' and picnicking with her boyfriend down in the creek, when this raving lunatic leapt down the embankment and nearly landed on her meringues. He shooed them away, but not before she saw him super-glue himself to the underside of the bridge. When she asked him what he was doing, he said he was waiting for the creek to flood so he'd drown."

"And what happened then?" said the audience.

"She pointed out to him that it was January, and that if he was lucky he might get washed away in May. If not, he could be there until July!"

Belchfire took another swig of his lager.

"Of course, she also pointed out to him that he would have starved to death by then, so he had a change of heart and told her to go and get help."

The audience waited expectantly while Belchfire had another swig.

"Of course the whole town turned out to have a look. They crowded onto the bridge, the bridge collapsed, and seventeen people two pigs and a dog fell to their deaths."

There was a sharp intake of breath from the audience. "Go-onn! Did they really?"

Belchfire picked up his pipe from the bar of the Wudgi Arms, and turned to leave.

"No, of course not. I went down there on my own with a tin of solvent, and soaked him free."

As he reached the door, Belchfire turned back to look at his bemused audience, and shook his head. Some people would believe anything!

The Witching Wars of Wudgi

The trouble started when Mrs. O'Malley went out to tend her vegetables, only to find that her zucchini's had turned into watermelons. She stood and scratched her head for a while, prodded a couple of melons with her foot, (as if by that very action they would change back into zucchini's), then scratched her head again.

They had been zucchini's yesterday - or at least, she thought they had. They had *always* been zucchini's! Mrs. O'Malley was famous for her zucchini's, because contrary to the laws governing most vegetable gardens, which were that *the vegetables shall grow within the circumscribed space allotted to them by the vegetable grower,* Mrs. O'Malley's vegetables, and especially her zucchini's, tended to run amok, growing out under the picket fence, across the pavement and into the road.

Tourists would come to marvel at her zucchini's, standing well back mind you, into the road, so as not to infringe upon their space. There was something arrogant about them; they were self possessed, strutting zucchini's, demanding more living room than the O'Malley had wanted them to have.

Put them in uniforms and you would have heard the stomp of the jackboots, the growl of the Panzers, and the cry "Lebensraum, Lebensraum" issuing from their little green mouths. Now they were gone - and in their place all these lumbering United Nations Water Melons, like a peace-keeping force that had moved in overnight.

Mrs. O'Malley looked thoughtful for a minute, and then glared over at her neighbour's property. Sarah Wartnose!!! Peering from behind a rhododendron bush was a wrinkly old woman that the O'Malley had crossed swords with before - on more than one occasion.

"Is that you, Wart? Come on out here you old witch. What have you done to my Zucchini's?'

The old woman emerged from behind the bush and cackled in delight.

"Your storm-troopers are gone, O'Malley. No more annexations of the common pavement; no more armed forays into the road, menacing peace loving neighbours and causing inconveniences. Gone, gone, gone! All mushy green pulp by now, I'd reckon."

"Why, you old hag, Warty. Two can play at that game. I have the auld Irish in me, and there's a few tricks that you heathens still have to learn."

O'Malley kicked a watermelon out into the road.

"And you can have these back - I don't want your sickly-sweet lolly water do-gooders on my property."

"It's not your property," Sarah spat back. It's a common thoroughfare, it's a pavement! It's for ordinary folks to walk on, not have to walk around because squatters have moved in! Your Zucchini's are a menace, Kate O'Malley."

"They're the only tourist attraction this town's got," Kate yelled back. "Now what are the tourists going to look at - your goitre!"

It was a terrible thing to say, and the O'Malley knew it. But Sarah Wartnose had quite a prominent goitre on her neck, and it was unmistakable.

"You'll burn in hell for that, Kate O'Malley. The old religion will find a cure for you - that's for sure!"

Sarah turned and dashed inside her little cottage and slammed the door. The O'Malley stood for a while, troubled. She knew the old Wart had a reputation as a witch hereabouts, and she was superstitious enough to give credence to it. Well, she'd have to fight fire with fire.

The next morning Sarah Wartnose wandered out into her garden, only to give out a yell and rush back indoors. One of her two cockerels had been turned into a black cat! So the O'Malley had fired the first shot. Sarah would have to brew up a potion.

Next door, the O'Malley wandered out, gave out a yell and rushed back indoors. Her black cat had been turned into a cockerel. The old witch! O'Malley would have to brew up a potion.

Over the next few weeks Wudgi folk began to get the feeling that something funny was going on. There was nothing specific that they could put their fingers on, but a number of unconnected events were quite out of the ordinary.

One evening, at Angus McSoufflé's Restaurant, the frogs' legs jumped out of the soup and skittered around the tables, giving the Mayor's wife a nasty turn when one hopped down the front of her bra and had to be fished out by the waiter with a soup ladle.

"Must have been too fresh," muttered McSoufflé. "Lucky they weren't still attached to the frogs."

Then there was the snake plague. Wudgi usually got its share of snakes in season, but nothing like

65

what descended on the town that particular year. The funny thing was that they weren't the usual brown snakes, but a multi-striped variety that looked as if they'd been manufactured in a lolly shop, and someone had got the recipe wrong.

The first the town knew of it was when Cora Littledove went shopping in the local store, and Fred Feeble suddenly said to her: "Don't be alarmed, Cora, but you have a snake wrapped around each ankle!"

Cora let out a shriek and galloped out of the shop with her knees further apart than they'd been since she won the splits championship in Convent School. Down by the creek, snakes were wriggling out of the mud and heading for the town in their hundreds, and it took a concerted effort by Captain Belchfire with the town's Fire Truck to run them all over in the main street before they caused any more alarm.

Everyone was edgy after this, and the vicar went around muttering about plagues of locusts and the end of the world. And that was before the bats!

It just happened that the hundredth anniversary of the building of the clock tower onto the Wudgi Town Hall was coming up, and some of the town's dignitary's, and some from the Progress Association, had decided to hold a little ceremony up in the belltower behind the clock, to re-dedicate the clock for the next hundred years.

Before the ceremony they had all assembled in the supper room, suitably attired, and prepared to make the rather hazardous ascent. His Worship, Ralph 'Rough' Red, was there in all his sartorial splendour, complete with chain of office, waistcoat, and a wig that his 90-year old mother had put through the washing machine and shrunk. Consequently, his head looked somewhat disorganised in relation to the rest of him.

Mrs Blithe-Brown was there of course, sniffing in that rather superior way that she had, that it was a good job that they only did this once every hundred years, because the climb to the belltower was so exhausting.

"Now, Maude, you complained about the exact same thing last time," said Jim Mopandle, grinning. Mrs Blithe-Brown sniffed, and ignored him.

"Now ladies, be very careful on the old staircase," said Angus McSoufflé, who was leading the party. "It's very narrow, very steep, and very old. There's probably a lot of dust up there, and there may be the odd mouse. Please don't be alarmed if there is; and no sudden movements. We'll proceed in single file."

He opened the small access door, and the group proceeded through. With His Worship trailing McSoufflé, the rest followed in line, fourteen in all.

The only person that had been up those stairs in the previous fifty years was Alistair Herringbone, the keeper of the clock, whose job it was to ascend those stairs once every twelve weeks to slap great dobs of grease on the giant cogs and bearings, to protect them from the weather. He also had to wind the clock, which he did, with a gigantic key. Then he would test the huge bell, which boomed out on the hour, and, with his head ringing, he would then go downstairs to fill out his application for sick leave for the next twelve weeks.

Old Alistair was stone deaf from the bell, and could never hear the Town Clerk telling him that his sick leave was denied. So the council put up with it, and paid him anyway.

"Oooh! I think I heard a mouse!" said Mrs. Harkpea, the Progress Association's secretary.

"Don't tell Angus, he'll make soup out of it and serve it up at his restaurant," muttered Jim Mopandle, not without a degree of truth.

McSoufflé was right into innovative cuisine.

After brief halts on the two landings, to enable the ladies to get their breath, the party eventually found itself gathered on a platform between the bell, and the workings of the clock, high above the main street of Wudgi.

The vicar had taken up his position, and opened his prayer book to begin, when a strange sound filled the air, like a beating of wings. Suddenly Mrs. Blithe-Brown looked up at Mrs. Harkpea and said, in horror - "I don't remember you wearing a hat, Sarah!"

"I didn't," said Mrs Harkpea, putting her hand up to feel what this strange thing was that had settled on her head.

"It's a bat!" yelled the vicar, and suddenly the air was filled with little black bodies and beating wings, and the shrieks and screams of the Re-Dedication Committee.

There must have been five hundred of them, and in the confusion Mrs. Blithe-Brown ended up straddled across the bell, the vicar got caught up between two cogs in the clock and had to be rescued later by the E.F.S., and Mrs. Harkpea somehow ended up on the outside of the clock, dangling from the hour hand.

There were committee members leaping everywhere in panic, and only McSoufflé kept his head, and stuffed as many bats as he could manage into a big plastic bag. The service was abandoned, and on the basis of every man and woman for themselves, the party found its way back to the Mayor's Chambers where they each had a double scotch from His Worship's private stock.

"It's those two witches," sobbed Mrs Harkpea. "They've been at it for days - witchcraft! They're trying to outdo each other."

Thus did the town find out about the O'Malley and Wartnose argument!

"There should be some sort of a council ruling about the practice of witchcraft in Wudgi," Mrs Blithe-Brown sniffed to the Mayor. She was unable to sit down, largely because the insides of her thighs were still vibrating from the clock-tower bell, which had chosen rather a delicate moment to strike the hour.

"I don't think the town elders thought too much about witchcraft," replied Mayor Red, "and if we tried to pass anything like that - in this day and age - we'd be laughed out of the Local Government Association."

"What about building regulations - operating a

business for gain in a residential zone?" The speaker was Wally Withers, occasional building inspector for Wudgi.

"But is it a business," sighed 'Rough' Red. "They could say they're just cooking up soup!"

"Not with earwigs, batwings and essence of flea," sniffed Mrs Blithe-Brown in admonition.

"It doesn't matter. Even that's covered by the cottage industry ruling," said Red.

"Hygiene regulations then. Cooking up potions in unsanitary cauldrons! We could make that stick."

"Unlikely. We'd have to find out what use the potions were being put to first, and they're hardly likely to tell us."

The meeting came to a close without any real conclusion being arrived at. The only resolution was that the Re-dedication Service was to be postponed until the faithful Herringbone could be despatched into the tower to clear out the rest of the bats.

That night two figures crept silently through the dusk, heading towards the two warring cottages on the outskirts of Wudgi. The figures were those of two men; the vicar, Reverend Cherub, and Angus McSoufflé, the town's only restaurateur. Under their arms they carried plastic bags filled with items of some bulk. On the other side of a hedge, the men halted and changed.

"I'm not sure that I should have let myself in for this," muttered the vicar.

"Of course you should - it's doing God's work. He'll thank you for it when you get up there," whispered Angus.

In her tiny kitchen Sarah Wartnose was humming a strange little tune as she stuffed a glutinous mixture into a huge cauldron over the old stove. Suddenly the back door flung open, and there, in the doorway, stood the Devil. In each hand he held two wriggling bats, and above the goat-like face was a pair of horns.

Sarah looked at him for a long moment.

"And about time, too! I could have done with those half an hour ago. The soup's ruined!"

In the cottage next door the O'Malley was sweeping up with an old-fashioned whisk broom. Suddenly the door flew open, and a strange apparition in a long black gown tripped over the step and fell sprawling on the floor, meanwhile releasing his grip on a dozen or so bats that immediately sought refuge, skittering around the room.

"Well, this is a surprise, McSoufflé! I didn't think your restaurant did Take-Away."

The entire exercise was an abject failure. Well, not quite. After listening to each woman's complaints, the two took the stories back to the council where a meeting was held well into the night. At the end of it the council ruled that the O'Malley's vegetable garden was to be listed as a tourist attraction for the town, and thus offered protection from the depredations of her neighbour; and in a special initiative, council undertook to underwrite the costs of medical treatment for Sarah Wartnose's goitre.

In time, Wudgi once again settled back into its lethargy, and no more stirrings were heard from the witches of Wudgi.

The Funeral of Zacariah Cribb

Zacariah Cribb was something of an institution around Wudgi. The town's only mortician, it was rumoured that his great-great-grandfather had set off from Melbourne in the 1850's in search of the goldfields at Ballarat, only to take a left instead of a right at Moonee Ponds, and end up, some weeks later, in the mid north of South Australia. Here, Instead of gold, he found scarlet fever, and commenced to make a viable living digging graves for six shillings each, with another two bob thrown in for filling them in again once the new owners had taken up residence. Thus did the Cribb family become undertakers!

The last of the breed, old Zacariah, had been plying his tophatted trade for as long as any of the locals could remember, and had in fact buried so many of the town's old timers that there was no-one left who could remember when he hadn't been around. Some of the wits around Wudgi called him: *"The Man who Buried a Town"*, as indeed he had.

With no close friends or confidants, it was inevitable that the myths would build up around him, and there was no shortage of these. The stories were usually shared over a beer at The Wudgi Arms on a Saturday night, when the farmers came in to quench their week-long thirsts.

There had been the case of the Malone family of Cotter's Farm. (Isn't it remarkable how the locals always know farms by the name of the previous inhabitants? Due to some perverse rural law, the Farm is now known as Malone's farm, as the Gantwee's are the current tenants).

But this aside; Molly Malone had been experimenting with toilet cleaners at the time, or so Fred Feeble of the town store said, because she had bought five different types the week before, and had complained at the time that the usual one didn't get the stains out once the goats and sheep had wandered through. And that was the last anyone saw of her - alive that is.

The story goes that she had doused the toilet pretty well with one kind of powder, added a dash of a liquid brand, then called her husband to have a look at what was happening in their loo because it was going all sorts of colours. Grandpa couldn't resist a look either, and then young Billy got curious as well, seeing all the oldies peering into the porcelain. Seamus Malone frowned at the bubbling cauldron in the pit of his porcelain, and taking another packet marked *"CAUTION - USE WITH CARE"* added a good 200 grams to the stew below.

Some days later, in the Wudgi Infirmary, four-year old Billy was being pressed to explain what had happened to his parents.

"Well - *Boom!* That's what it said," remarked young Billy, confused. "*Boom!* And all this green cloud jumped up, an' Mum an' Dad an' Gramps just stood there, an' sort uv slowly fell over in a heap!"

Billy had taken off in shock and horror, but not before he had got a good whiff of pure Ammonia gas that knocked him out by the time he got to his own room.

Thus it was that the Malone family was not discovered until the next day, when Col Springett happened by looking for an old bit for his new horse.

The Malone's were all as stiff as a board by this time, and when Zacariah arrived to do his stuff, it was a bit of a problem, getting them to the cart. And that was the crux of the story.

"Barry Badgeworth - the one by the old creek - not one of the Badgeworths of Addlebury - No! Barry Badgeworth swears that when he happened to come around the back from the hay paddock, there was old Cribb in his Top Hat and tails, pushing Molly Malone along on a sack truck, standing up mind you, to the old hearse he uses for pick-ups, then tipping her into the back and sliding her in head first.

Then he went back for Seamus, stuck his feet on the sack truck just the same, wheeled him out and up to the hearse; only Scamus had one arm sticking out at right angles to his body, and it looked as if he was giving Zacariah a guided tour. Then to top it off, old Gramps fell off the sack trolley three times on the way to the hearse, and ended up bending in half, so Cribb had to drag him the rest of the way by his feet. And you know what? All this time old Cribb's whistling and singing to himself, and guess what he was singing? God's truth, it was "Danny Boy", and the Malone's being good Catholic God fearing Irish folk, too. Bloody shame!"

Then of course, there was the tortured tale of the Mayor of Wudgi, who as part of his Municipal duties had got pie-eyed after the Wudgi Pig-Fest, and had stopped in at the funeral parlour to settle a council bill for the burial of an itinerant. Unfortunately for him, he was none too steady on his legs and had fallen rather heavily once inside the door, cracking his head on a low beam.

Zacariah had ambled out somewhat later to find an unexpected but not unwelcome commission lying on his rug, smelling rather like a three-day old corpse, courtesy of the Pigs.

Zacariah took a few tentative sniffs and realised that there wasn't a moment to lose. Before you could say Jack Robinson he had his Worship's trousers and jacket off, and had wandered out the back to look for a suitable outfit to bury him in.

The Mayor woke up, saw the coffin next to him, looked down at his bare legs and shirt-tails and with a yell that would have woken the dead in the Wudgi cemetery took off through the door and down the main street of the town. Old Cora Littledove, a lifelong spinster, said it almost gave her a heart attack. As it was, she ended up with a black eye from the telescope that walloped her as she jumped up in fright. Whenever she told the story after that, a certain coyness made her omit the part about the telescope - people might have got ideas.

Anyway, the stories about old Zacariah Cribb were legion, even to the one told to the young children of Wudgi, that underneath the floor of the undertaker's was a pit that led directly to hell, and that on Walpurgis night he could be seen dancing to the flickering shadows of the hell-fire pit, with all the currently resident corpses jerking in time to some unearthly music.

So after all that, it seems strange now to have to tell you about what happened when old Zacariah finally died himself, and how his own funeral entered the realms of local folklore.

It all started at the funeral of Elsie Whitlow, beloved wife of John Whitlow, mother to Deborah, Jillian and Craig, and grandmother to Jason, Abigail, Angie-Lee, Nicholas and Trevor.

The service at the graveside was in full swing, if one can thus describe a burial, and there was a certain amount of tension in the air because it was generally believed that old Elsie and Zacariah Cribb had once had a bit of a 'fling' in their youth, and he had never got over the final rejection when she went off and married a locksmith.

No doubt, if there had been another mortician in the town, John Whitlow would have taken his business elsewhere. But Addlebury was seventeen kilometres away, and in small country towns there is always the problem of local patronage. One must not be seen to be disloyal to ones neighbors.

So John Whitlow gritted his teeth, and put up with it. When Zacariah took up a position at the foot of the grave, Whitlow was beside himself. He didn't dare make a scene at his wife's funeral, so he let it pass. But the other mourners could hear quite well the grinding of teeth, and they had no doubt about where the sound was coming from. John was not amused.

Just as the minister was saying 'ashes to ashes', Zacariah gave out a muffled groan, and toppled, like a felled oak, straight into the pit. There he lay, sprawled I might add, across the coffin of the good lady Elsie Whitlow. John Whitlow gave out a growl of rage. This was really going too far!

He strode to the edge of the grave, quivering in anger.

"You get out of there this minute, Zacariah Cribb, or do I have to drag you out?"

There was no answer from the undertaker, who appeared to be embracing the coffin at the bottom of the hole in some orgasm of despair.

"Leave my wife alone, you perverted old bugger," roared the locksmith, finally losing what control he had left. Still the undertaker did not move.

"Ahem," said the vicar, feeling that perhaps he

should try to regain control over what, to that point, had been really rather a nice service. "Perhaps Mr. Cribb is feeling unwell," the vicar ventured. "I suggest we leave him for a bit, and perhaps finish the service; then we can work out what to do with him."

"What! ... What! ... finish the service ... finish the service, with that bluebeard draped over my wife, and her not even decently in the ground yet," blustered John Whitlow, the veins standing out on his forehead in rather an alarming fashion. The vicar suddenly remembered something about discretion being the better part of valour, and backed off a safe distance to consult his hymnal.

"Get out of there, Cribb, or I'm coming in," yelled Whitlow, at the recumbent body of his foe.

The younger members of the congregation began to titter at the incongruity of it all, and then suddenly the Misses Whitlow burst into hysterical tears and the graveside became a shambles.

To the rescue came a measured voice from the rear, and pushing his way through the milling throng with an air of calm authority, Dr. Derwent Pater-Proby appeared at the edge of the orifice, and looked down, gravely.

"I think I'd better check him out," he said, and

hoisted himself with some difficulty into the hole. After a few moments he looked up.

"I'm afraid our Mr. Cribb is beyond my help."

There was a deathly silence.

"You mean he's dead," barked the locksmith in disbelief. "How dare he... I mean, what a moment to choose. He did it deliberately!"

Whitlow paced backwards and forwards along the side of the grave, knocking little showers of earth into the pit and over the doctor. Suddenly he erupted.

"He's buggered off with my wife!"

All hell broke loose at this, and for some minutes there was wailing, screaming, gnashing of teeth, and muttered platitudes, all vying with each other to be heard as the funeral party gave in to hysterics. The vicar wrung his hands together.

"What are we to do? Oh what; what are we to do?"

"Well, you can get *him* out of there for a start," yelled Whitlow, quite beside himself.

"Do you really think that's such a good idea," said the vicar. "I mean - this leaves the town without a funeral director - for the first time in a hundred and forty years. Maybe it would be better just to leave him where he is and just... and just..."

"What... just what? - fill in the hole," barked Whitlow. "Not with my wife you don't! Right! That's it. Get my wife out of there. She's not staying here."

On this, he jumped into the hole, wrestled the doctor to one side, prodded Zacariah with his foot until he slid sideways and off the coffin, and then bent down to wrestle with his dearly beloved wife's mortal remains.

Late reports stated that Whitlow and a few other burly fellows were last seen tramping across country with a coffin on their shoulders, heading in the general direction of Addlebury.

"What about him," said the doctor, when the rest of the group had dispersed, and there was only the vicar, looking somewhat dazed by it all.

"Can you sign the death certificate," asked the vicar.

The doctor nodded.

"A bit unconventional, but yes, I think we can sort that out."

"Then start shovelling," said the vicar, "and I'll read the service."

And so it was that Wudgi lost its only funeral director, the last of a long line of Cribbs.

The Devereaux of Dingbat Mansions

Elias Carbunkle was once the story-teller of
Wudgi. What he didn't remember about the many
inhabitants who had come and gone over the years
wasn't worth knowing; or that's what folks said,
anyway. He seemed to have lived there forever,
always in his wheelchair, whiling away the autumn
days of his life on the shaded kerb between the fish
and chip shop and the police station. Not that he
told many stories in the latter years of his life,
mind you, or he would be telling you this one, and
I would be spared the effort. One horrendous day
in the winter of 1992 finished all that. By the time
the West Coast Bus had rolled through the town on
that fateful day, Elias had told his last story.

It was a bit nippy that morning, minus six
degrees to be exact, and Elias had got it into his
head that perhaps a cherry brandy at the Wudgi
Arms Hotel might just melt the ice that was
forming in his beard. He had wheeled his chair
carefully to the kerb, then turned it 180 degrees,
having found by long experience that it was easier
to negotiate Wudgi's kerbs backwards than
forwards. As luck would have it, just as his chair
lurched into the road in reverse, Jake Peddler drove

his West Coast Bus at a fair clip along the main street, heading for points north and west.

Now Buses tend to be rather pneumatic beasts, constantly sucking and blowing air in and out of their various orifices, and creating occasionally the equivalent of a whirlwind in their wake. On this particular morning Jake was running late, and was less than cautious in his steering. Thus he approached dangerously close to where Elias Carbunkle was celebrating his complicated maneouvres in the wheelchair.

Suddenly, Elias heard a roar, and felt an enormous suction seize hold of his wheelchair and perambulate it in reverse out into the road behind the bus. There was a sudden jerk, and Elias was instantly barrelling backwards up the main street of Wudgi at something approaching 50 kilometres per hour, his wheelchair firmly secured to a luggage hook on the back of the bus.

His first instinct was to throw his hands up in the air and shout for help. No sound would come, however. It takes breath to shout, and just at that moment Elias didn't seem to have any.

Further along the main street Mrs. Harkpea, out for a bit of shopping, observed him waving at her. She waved politely back, and smiled.

"Oh, isn't that nice. Old Mr. Carbunkle is going for a trip. It must be one of those Old-Timer tours that they've put on for the elderly citizens. It's about time he got away from Wudgi for a while."

Next to her, Mrs. Blithe-Brown stopped and frowned.

"That's rather an unorthodox way to travel. Surely the bus isn't full; perhaps he's on a special fare," she sniffed.

The bus disappeared around the corner, heading north, and Elias with it. As the bus accelerated to 80 kilometres an hour and headed out over the bridge, the bearings in his wheelchair began to make a high pitched, whining sound, and Elias clung grimly to the arm rests and began to mutter what might have been a prayer - (if Elias had been a religious man, that is).

In the event, he was actually reciting the first chapter of his wheelchair service manual, the bit that said:

"...given a reasonable amount of care, your new Hubble-Bubble Wheelchair will give you years of service, and a mobility that will be the envy of your friends."

Once out of the town the bus picked up to a hundred k's, and Elias practiced holding his breath, then letting it go, and then holding it again, every time they hit a bump in the road. Meanwhile he felt his beard turn into a block of ice, and by the time they were halfway to Port Augusta he couldn't feel himself anymore.

The Police patrol that pulled the bus over just outside Augusta had been startled to see an old man sitting glassy eyed in a wheelchair, with both tyres flat, and bits of rubber flying off what was left of them with monotonous regularity.

Jake Peddler accompanied the officers to the rear of his bus with trepidation. Elias wasn't sayin' nothin'.

"You got a licence for this thing?" said Constable Pullworthy. He took out a little pad and began to write.

"Are you aware, sir, that you have two flat tyres?"

There was a long silence. The only sign of life that Elias was capable of at that moment was a rather demented look about the eyes.

In a louder, angrier tone, Pullworthy went on:

"Do you know the penalty for not wearing a seat belt, sir? What have you got to say for yourself old man."

Elias was beyond saying anything. His hands

were iced onto the armrests, and his jaw appeared to be locked - if indeed it was there at all under his ice-bound beard. He certainly couldn't feel it.

"You realise that I'm also going to have to give you a defect sticker for this conveyance. That means that you must leave this vehicle by the side of the road, and arrange to have it collected later."

He paused. "If I see you riding about in this before the defect is taken off, you may be liable to arrest! Now; if you ask the bus driver nicely, he might give you a lift into Port Augusta."

At this, the bus driver, Jake Peddler, suddenly found his tongue.

"Of all the cheek! And he never even paid for a ticket in the first place!"

As Jake bent to unhook the stowaway and his conveyance from the bus, he became aware of a number of sounds emanating from the occupant of the wheelchair. The first was a sound like the breaking of glass as the ice cracked around Elias's fingers, releasing them from the armrests. The next was a low gurgling sound way back in the stowaway's throat, which turned into what might have been a low growl, culminating in a sound halfway between a roar and a howl as Elias suddenly lunged from his chair and bit Peddler's ear off, before falling insensible to the ground.

To say that the bus driver was perturbed at this turn of events would be an understatement. In fact, he was rather peeved. Actually, 'peeved' doesn't quite cover it. Peddler himself used more appropriate language to describe the demise of his ear, now spat out in the road, by jumping up and down seriously on one foot, and letting go with a varago of expletives mainly beginning with 'f'.

Well, since then, Elias has taken up his old position between the fish and chip shop and the police station, and he whiles away his days as before. But he's never spoken a word since - (unless you count 'pthaw-pthaw' as a word, accompanied by a spitting sound). Now there is a chain permanently attaching his wheelchair to the old hitching rail outside the police station, and all thoughts of cherry brandy on cold days have long gone from his head.

Anyway, that wasn't the story I set out to tell you. I just relate it to illustrate the point that Elias Carbunkle was a far better storyteller than I, and what follows is one of his old stories, which he used to tell a lot better because he knew the various protagonists. It's a pity you didn't turn up here before he became catatonic!

In his much younger days, and that was back in the '40's I might add, the young Elias was in service as a sort of 'boots' to the Devereaux family, who occupied Dingbat Mansions, the estate by the Adelaide Road. They were a mysterious family to the Wudgi locals. Rarely seen in public, they had claims to the aristocracy, and employed a butler, a cook, a kitchen maid, a parlourmaid, an above-the-stairs maid, an under-the-stairs maid, a pantry maid, a gardener, a gardener's assistant and a boots. Most of the servants, except for the butler and cook, lodged in the gardener's cottage, while the gardener slept under the rhododenrons, and his assistant in the bough of an oak tree behind the mansion.

The family itself consisted of Sir Barley de Water Devereaux; his wife, Lady Mona Gripe de la Whiskey Devereaux; their son, the Hon. Barkwit Lilygathering Polehead Devereaux, and a daughter called Toots.

Sir Barley held a hereditary Baronetcy, and was closely related to Earl Wuuf of Lear, the Caramel Buttonhole Merchant King. Earl Wuuf was fabulously wealthy; his caramel buttonholes had so taken on in the 'naughty nineties' that it was said there was not a garment in England that did not fall revealingly apart as a result of the buttonholes having been chewed out in the night. This being the case, Sir Barley had always entertained an expectation of huge wealth being his, once Earl Wuuf had shuffled off this mortal coil.

But Earl Wuuf had showed no real inclination to go. In fact, by 1950, when Earl Wuuf turned eighty, he was pronounced by his doctors as 'good for another thirty years or so', at which Sir Barley had taken his family off to Australia, built the twenty seven room Mansion at Wudgi, and settled down to wait.

In 1955, while hunting giant bilbeys in the swamp south of Wudgi, Sir Barley had unaccountably disappeared. Various rumours flew about Wudgi at the time, none of them substantiated, and Sir Barley's remains were never found. But it was variously rumoured that (1) he had been taken by a Dingbat - (the local version of a Bunyip; and it was only then that the Mansion began to be called Dingbat Mansions); (2) that he had gone snorkelling for newts to add to his frog collection, and had been sucked under, or taken by a giant newt; (3) that agents of a cousin of Earl Wuuf had assassinated him to redirect the expected legacy to the cousin; and (4) that Lady Devereaux had eaten him as a result of straitened circumstances, brought about by the long wait for the legacy. But no-one really knew.

Barkwit, who was by this time nineteen, became Barkwit Lilygathering Polehead Devereaux, Seventeenth Baron Winkley, K.G., P.T.O., L.P.G., P.M.G. etc. Far from being cut off from Earl Wuuf's millions, the old Earl was said to have always been fond of the lad, and made it plain that his fortune would be heading in the direction of Australia regardless.

Now Barkwit was more of an adventurous type than his father, and thought to venture out to see the world once he had attained his majority. Elias Carbunkle had been working as boots since 1948, and was party to what went on at the time.

"Lady Whiskey-breath - because that's what I called her," said Elias, "was most concerned that Barkwit should not leave the safety of the mansion until Earl Wuuf's fortune was safely secured. But Barkwit rebelled.

One day, in 1962, he walked along the main street and down to the old stables, and stood for some time looking at the statue of Jack Turnip, sitting in the horse trough with the bucket on his head. He seemed fascinated by it, and said to me:

"Oh, that I should one day be as famous as Turnip! I have ambition, Carbunkle; I have pride! I shall walk tall through the everglades of life and cast caution to the winds. Dash it all! I shall raise the name of Devereaux to men's lips, and then leap to new heights before they have the chance to drink. They will call me Baron Bold, or Baron Daring, or Baron of the Braveheart..."

"...or Baron Winkley, I thought," said Elias. "Of course, Barkwit was all of five foot four and raving mad."

"Tomorrow, Elias, I shall defy my mother once more. I shall go to the chemist!"

"He did, too," said Elias. "He bought some arsenic for the wasps and tried to poison his mother. Luckily for him she was so pickled on whiskey that it had no effect.

But his rebellion continued, and each day he went a little further and a little further, until one day he went to Melbourne and never came back. They said he'd been run over by a steam train or some such thing, but no-one really knew. Like his father, he just disappeared!

By 1975, Dingbat Mansions was like a morgue.

"The butler and cook had gone, so had the kitchen maid, the parlour maid, the above-the-stairs maid, the below-the-stairs maid and the gardener. They'd run off together, actually, and were never replaced. Toots had married the gardener's assistant, and they had gone off to live in Toorak. I was still boots, and I was still there when the lawyers, *Fiddler, Diddler, Wriggler & Barp* came to tell us that Earl Wuuf had died, aged 105, and had left his money to Barkwit. No sooner had they left than this ragged looking tramp staggered in the door, and gasped out, "Mother... I'm home. I got a little held up in Calcutta!"

Lady Mona took one look at him and said:

"Who the bloody hell are... oh! Barkwit? Now you wouldn't forget your old *mother,* would you!"

"There was something in the way she said it," said Elias, "that made Barkwit take a step backwards. They sort of circled around each other, warily, as if neither of them were too sure of themselves."

Elias was quiet for a moment, as if he was remembering that vivid scene.

"Of course, *I knew it wasn't Barkwit!* Barkwit had been only five foot four, this fellow was six foot one. Anyway, I'd seen this fellow before. He'd been a lawyers clerk in the office of *Fiddler, Diddler & Co.* about ten years before."

"Didn't you say something," I asked, surprised.

"What about his poor mother; was she taken in by it?"

"Not for a moment, but as it wasn't his mother - (as he would have known if he had really been her son) - she couldn't say much, really! It was Peggy the pantry maid, who'd taken the mother's place after Lady Whiskey breath had gone searching the swamp for Sir Barley, and disappeared. No - the Devereaux were all gone!"

"So what happened to the inheritance?"

"We split it up between us. How do you think an old coot in a wheelchair came to be the richest landlord in Wudgi?"

The Rustik Flok Concert

Jud Blackhand turned up in Wudgi in 1974. He seemed to appear from nowhere; that was the general perception. Other folks, with more of a stake in the town, opined that he was a messenger from hell, or at least from regions in that general area, because his effect on the town was far out of proportion to his humble occupation.

Jud was a printer. The first the townfolk knew about him was that he had secured a lease on the old gardener's cottage on the Dingbat estate, thrown up a shed, and from that shed was heard the wheeze and thump of an old platen that began to churn out advertising leaflets for the General Store, and invoice books for the local tradesmen.

The trouble with Jud was that he was dyslectic. As often as not the items listed on his various productions had little, if anything, in common with the products advertised. The spelling was wrong, whole items appeared upside down, at times it was necessary to hold the leaflet up to a mirror to read it, and for the better educated of Wudgi Crossing the entire appearance of Jud's efforts was an anathema.

Mrs. Delaney would ride her three-wheeler

breathlessly up the pavement and into Fred Feeble's shop. Bowling over the washing powder display, and waving Jud's latest missive in Fred's face, she would demand angrily:

"What the blazes is *'500 Gramp Bunions?'* And what are *'Disposable Ravers?'* And since when did you stock 250 gram *'Tuns of Beetrot?'*

Mrs. Delaney was an ex-school teacher, and would be utterly dismayed every time one of these little flyers landed in her letterbox.

"Now, now, Mrs. Delaney. No need to get upset. I know it's a bit of a problem, but a bad printer is better than no printer at all. At least I can put out lists of Specials now, I couldn't before Jud turned up."

"But really, Fred - *Bredd Crubbs, Plum Jum, Mushroom Piecles and Stums?* He's driving me mad, Fred. He's destroying the language. You've got to do something about it!"

But Fred had no intention of doing anything about it. He had noticed that the more errors Jud produced in his Specials List, the more notice people took of it, and the more produce he sold. He was doing very well, thank you, and Jud could keep on making his multiple errors as far as he was concerned. Besides which, the only other printer was in Addlebury, and to go to Addlebury for anything was unthinkable to Wudgi folk.

The only businessman that really took exception to Jud's shortcomings was Angus McSoufflé, who was a stickler for exactitude. When his Menus came back, listing such oddities as *Oisters Kill Patrick, Fishermans Busket,* and *Craps Suzetts,* he sent them back to be printed again. The trouble was that by the time he had even bothered to read them, the Menus had been sitting on the tables for a week. He'd wondered why no-one by the name of 'Patrick' ever frequented his Restaurant!

The second time around Jud supplied him with *Horses Douvers,* and *Ess' Cargoes,* not to mention the infamous *Smorgasbroad,* and *Pouffet - the* latter of which almost got him in trouble with the anti-discrimination people. So that was it, McSoufflé would have nothing further to do with *Blackhand Press,* and took the extreme step of going to Addlebury for his printing.

1974 was a funny year for music. Pop music was in a state of flux after the demise of the super groups of the sixties, and everyone seemed to be on the lookout for what was going to be *the next big thing.* I mention this in passing, because although Wudgi to that point had not suffered a huge exposure to Rock & Roll, Folk music, or even Country music, events that unfolded that summer brought with them a legacy that Wudgi would never live down.

Breezing into town one hot summer's day came an itinerant musician - and I use that word loosely - called Jakov Wopuvic, a Ukrainian journeyman folk singer.

Wopuvic was what you might call a twisted genius. He played a treat on something that looked like a three stringed zither, and extracted the most excruciating notes out of a comb wrapped in tissue paper. He was in league with other 'folkies' who plied their trade on the road, playing to anyone who was crazy enough to listen. Wopuvic was the advance guard of this group, sent on to spy out likely venues for a Rustic Folk Concert.

When Jakov blew into Wudgi, and took in the marvellous Imaginary Golf Course on the other side of the creek, he could visualise a huge open-air concert of folk music, and decided to advertise before the others got there. So almost his first stop was the gardener's cottage with the sign *"Bluckhand Pres" on* the fence.

Jakov got along with Jud like a house on fire.

They spent half an hour huddled over a pipe stuffed with little green heads, and two minutes composing the poster. That came out as follows:

TO BE HELD ON
DECEMBER 15

AT THE IMAJINARY GOLF CORSE, WUDGI CROSSING

The Great Wudgi
RUSTIK FLOK
MUSIC FESTIVEL

Perhaps I should explain here that the Imaginary Golf Course was the brainchild of Jim Mopandle, the president of the Wudgi Progress Association, who felt that an imaginary golf course was better than no golf course at all, and so used his influence with the council to have the necessary signs erected. But it was basically wasteland on the other side of the creek, with a few holes poked in it using the blunt end of a walking stick. The advantage was that if you didn't like the holes provided, you could poke some in for yourself.

Jakov seemed quite happy with the printed product, and went off with a bundle of posters under his arm. He proceeded to paste them to every lamp-post and power pole in Wudgi, then jumped onto an ancient motor scooter and covered the various roads leading in and out of Wudgi for a distance of ten kilometres.

Coincidentally at this time, a chartered coach full of American Tourists blundered into Wudgi after the driver had lost his way, and once there, couldn't seem to leave. First of all it was a flat tyre, then a fuel problem, and finally the gearbox packed up just as the coach was edging slowly over the bridge, leaving Wudgi cut off from the rest of the civilised world. Leaving the coach and looking blearily around, one was heard to observe:

"Where in tarnation are we? Is this the set of *'The Land That Time Forgot?'"*

The Coach driver was most apologetic.

"I'm really sorry, folks. This was the one place I was trying to avoid, but it looks as if we're going to be stuck here for a couple of days until I get the gearbox fixed, so we'll just have to make the best of it. There's a pub - tavern - down the road called 'The Wudgi Arms'. We might be able to get some of you in there for the night, or we might be able to use the Old Hall."

Grumbling, the tourists wandered off the bus, dragging overnight bags with them, and one foolhardy gent took his golf clubs gingerly out of the luggage compartment, determined to fit in a round of golf while they waited. This was Abe Spangle, the Head of *Raucous Records* in Memphis, Tennessee. He'd brought a couple of bodyguards with him, and they dutifully traipsed along beside him to the Imaginary Golf Course, when in fact they would have much rather joined the others on the way to the local 'tavern'.

On their arrival at the course, Abe looked around and scratched his head.

"Hey, these Aussies play it tough, don't they? It's all traps and roughs. Where are the fairways and the greens?"

Walt and Dicky were non-plussed. They all gazed around at the scrub and the salt-bush, the pools of brackish water, and the withered trees in the distance, and shrugged their shoulders.

"It looks like you have to slash your way through this one, boss. I'd use a crowbar and a cannon ball," said Walt, unenthusiastically.

"Even the holes are rough. Look at this - looks as if it was poked in with a walking stick."

Abe took a couple of trial swings, and bits of saltbush flew off in all directions. Suddenly there was a yell from over by the trees, and a shambling figure staggered towards them. He was dressed in a white dustcoat, and looked like a disarrayed chemist - which is what he was!

Horus Archibilus had been enjoying a bracing stroll amongst the pink-toed miniature zebras that seemed to congregate about him on these walks - (whenever he imbibed that mixture of mescaline and lysergic acid diethylamide that he kept for research purposes). Then suddenly, a golf ball had come winging its way through the trees and hit him ignobly on the forehead.

This in itself would not have dismayed him too much, but the pink-toed zebras had immediately been transformed into hairynosed wombats with purple and yellow feathers, and Horus was rather alarmed that the delicate balance of his hallucination had been upset forever.

"Here, what do you think you're doing," he yelled at the Americans, waving their golf ball in the air. "Have you paid your ground fees? What's the idea of using a real golf ball - and real golf clubs as well," he said indignantly, as he got closer and saw the golf bag full of its resplendent clubs.

"Who are you, Mac? Are you the greenkeeper? This course is a disgrace. Where are the fairways," Abe snorted back.

"Americans!" Horus expostulated. "This is an

Imaginary Golf Course for imaginary golfers, with imaginary clubs and imaginary golf balls."

Abe looked at Walt, and Dickey looked at Abe, then Walt looked at Dickey and Abe looked at Horus.

"Nuts!" he concluded, for the three of them.

Horus would have responded, but suddenly the drugs in his system told his legs to collapse, which they did, and he lay on his back, flailing his arms and yelling: "Caterpillars; hairy caterpillars!"

Suddenly everything was hairy to Horus. Hairy trees, hairy men, hairy rabbits with hairy teeth hovered over him, and looked at him with their hairy eyes. He looked in vain for the pink-toed miniature zebras - they had long gone.

Horus sat bolt upright and looked at the now horrified Americans with a fixed stare.

"Give me back my zebras", he yelled, and something in the tone of his voice made the three of them turn and run. Dragging the golf bag between them they didn't stop until they got back to the bridge, and it was on the bridge that Abe noticed, for the first time, the notice pasted up not three hours before by Jakov.

"What the frig is Rustik Flok?" said Walt.

"Rustik what," Abe replied. "Well, that takes

the cake. We get away from the *hairy caterpillar man* by the skin of our teeth, only to find that the whole town's off the planet. They've got a whole new type of music here that I've never heard of - Hey!!! Maybe we've stumbled onto the *next big thing.* Maybe this Flok is going to take the world by storm, and here we are, in on the ground floor. Dickey, you're the fix-it man. I want a full recording crew and outside studios set up here ready for this concert. *Raucous Records* is going to get first bite at this!"

Up at the Wudgi Arms the three men got into a huddle and borrowed the pub phone to make a few urgent calls to the outside world. But it's hard to keep anything a secret in Wudgi especially in the Wudgi Arms Hotel. Snippets of phone conversation were overheard by the drinkers and relayed between each other, and at this rush of interest by American tourists in a local event, it wasn't long before the local businessmen could see a dollar in the wind.

Angus McSoufflé was no exception. He could see his restaurant providing an outside catering service to thousands of the faithful, and in his minds eye he even coined generic names for the fare such as *Flok Burgers, Flok Dogs, Rustik Chips* and *Flokky Chicken in Rustik Boxes.* There was no end to McSoufflé's inventiveness when it came to making a buck.

Meanwhile, Abe had been having a re-think.

"Hey, Walt. What if *Raucous Records* actually sponsors the event - you know, we get our name on it right at the start. That way, if it turns out like 'Woodstock' or 'Monterey', then that's what people will remember - *'The Great Raucous Records Rustik Flok Concert.'*

Walt thought that was a great idea, so the two of them got down to scheming. It was agreed that they would have more of a bargaining position with this Jakov if they had a new poster mocked up, showing *Raucous Records* as the sponsors, and promising free publicity and subsequent record release. Thus it was that Walt found himself calling in at Blackhand Press, situated at the gardener's cottage on the Dingbat Estate.

Jud Blackhand seemed an affable enough fellow, and promised a thousand posters by the following day.

Abe was sitting in the beer garden of the Wudgi Arms, sipping a lager, when Walt finally rolled up with the posters.

"I don't think you're going to like it, boss,"

were his first apprehensive words to his employer.

Abe looked at him quizzically, then snatched one of the posters off him to read. At first he went white, then he seemed to choke a little, then his eyebrows knitted into a black frown. Abe was speechless for a few minutes, then muttered: "is this the same printer that did the original poster?"

Walt swallowed, and muttered: "Yes, it is."

"So, what you're telling me is that there's no such thing as *Rustik Flok Music*, only the demented spelling of a lunatic printer?"

"You said it, boss!"

For the next few minutes the air was filled with the sort of obscenities that are usually only heard in Memphis, Tennessee. But Abe was interrupted by the bus driver, announcing that the gearbox had been fixed, and they were now ready to roll!

There was no hesitation. Abe, Walt and Dickey made a rush for the bus, and were gone before the locals could realise that Wudgi's chance at International fame had gone with them.

The concert, as previously scheduled, went ahead, and the twenty-six foolhardy souls who composed themselves around the saltbush of the third tee were to regret that day forever. Jakov and his cronies served up the worst concoction of out-of time twanging on the strangest of strange instruments, before being pelted with half chewed *Flok Burgers* and bottles of *Rustik Kola* that McSoufflé had rushed up on special order by the thousand.

Luckily, McSoufflé's midnight suicide attempt was only half-hearted, and he survived the twelve dozen Oysters Kilpatrick that he swallowed that night. But his customers were eating Rustik fare for months to come.

Preserved in the dusty archives of the Wudgi Town Hall is a single copy of the poster that had made Abe Spangle's eyes bug out, and cost Wudgi some much needed publicity. Here it is:

Rorkus Rekords Prezennt

THE MUSSIC CRAYZ THATS
SWEPING THE WURLD!

The Grate Rorkus Rekords Rusdik Fluko Consert

to be hald at the
Imagginry Golff Curse
Wudgie Cruising
December 15th -

AND TO BE REEKORDED LYVE!!!

The Wudgi Tram

Two inches beneath the sealed surface of Wudgi's main street, there lies buried two long steel rails, the only remains of that glorious time when, for three days, Wudgi had its own tram. Local folk prefer to forget that those rails are still there, for reasons that will become clear.

Over the years since that experimental feat of engineering, the rails somehow became magnetised at right angles to the earth's field. As a result, shopping trolleys from the local store often run out into the road and gather in a cluster around the top end of what was once the terminus, at the top of the hill. Little boys on roller skates are dragged off the pavement, whooping, and forced to skate unwillingly down the hill, head on into the traffic. This has resulted in more than one pile up of catastrophic proportions. Even old Ebenezer Ratchitt, with his polio leg-irons, spent an uncomfortable night glued to the centre line in the driving rain, before he was mercifully struck by lightning and released from his ordeal.

"We're going to have to dig them up," fumed councillor Mopandle, after Esmerelda Ripperchest got her horse stranded in the middle of the road.

(Mopandle was known to be a little 'soft' on Esmerelda). "Blacksmith Harry Bellows had to come along and pry the horse's shoes off where it stood."

"That's all very well, Jim, but how are we going to pay for it? It'll tear up that nice bitumen surface we had to wait so long for. The time to do it was then, not now!"

The speaker was Mayor Ralph 'Rough' Red, in his third term as Mayor, and four times champion of the Wudgi Wineries Claret Guzzling Extravaganza.

"The cost can be offset by selling the rails for scrap," Mopandle replied. "I've heard that steel fetches $145 a ton. There must be a few tons in those old rails. They stretch for about four hundred and eighty yards if I remember correctly, ending up by the bridge over the creek. At three yards of double rail to the ton that will give us over twenty three thousand dollars."

"Yes, Jim. But resurfacing that main street will cost in the region of half a million. Where are we going to get that sort of money?"

There was no answer to that, as the Progress Association had exactly thirty-six dollars and fifty four cents in the kitty, and the vicar had earmarked that to weld a crack in the church bell.

"Well, I hope the town's public liability is up to date," said Mopandle, as a parting riposte. "Sure as eggs is eggs, there's going to be a major disaster one day, over those rails."

Jim was correct. There *was* a major disaster in the offing, one that not even he could have foreseen. But that is another story.

I'm here to tell you about the Wudgi Tram, and those halcyon days back in 1955 when the town's inhabitants thought that, at last, they were about to enter the twentieth century. It all came about with the arrival of Enrico Salvatore de la Forté, a Venezualan engineer of mixed Portuguese, French, Spanish and Italian forebears who stumbled into Wudgi Crossing one day on the end of a switch of Hazel, divining for water.

Once rested up after his ordeal of crossing the Imaginary Golf Course on foot – still the only living man to have accomplished this feat blindfolded – he turned his attention to the township of Wudgi and sought out its leading lights. This meant the vicar, the Reverend Holysmock, the Mayor, the Honourable Bill Outstanding, and the secretary of the Progress

Association of the time, Abigail Woolgathering. The Town Clerk of the time, Jeremiah Pickandle, (second cousin, twice removed from the later Jim Mopandle), was not present at that first meeting, though he played a significant part in subsequent events.

"It eez that I haf been primarily hengaged in the construction of a tramline for the past three years, along the banks of the Amazon river, in Argentina."

At this point, anyone with even a primary school knowledge of geography would have bailed out of any scheme of Enrico's, but in 1955, to the Wudgi luminaries, anywhere as exotic as South America was alien territory, the subject of hearsay and speculation only. The fact that the Amazon River ran through Brazil and not Argentina did not impinge upon their consciousness.

"Yeass! For twenty seven hundred miles, I haf built zis tramline, and it iss now one of the seventeen wonders of the civilized world. I could do ze same for Wudgi Crossing."

"Well, we haven't exactly got twenty seven hundred miles to play with," simpered the Reverend Holysmock. "In fact, at this stage, there's really only the main street, and as you can see, even that's not very big."

"Leave this to me, Bruce," the Mayor cut in. "You see Monsewer de la Forté, it's questionable whether or not Wudgi *needs* a tram. I mean, who would use it? The only place we could run it would be from the bridge, and up the hill into the main street. That's about a quarter of a mile. I know it's a bit of a hike up the hill, but it's only women with shopping bags who would see the need for it."

"Heggs-actly! Ze women wiv ze shopping. And ze delivery boys wiv deliveries to ze shops. And ze tourists who won't go anywhere unless zere is a public transport system."

"He's got a point there," said Miss Woolgathering, who was all for progress at any cost. "If we're ever going to grab a slice of the tourist trade, we need something like this." Then she played her ace card. "It would be one up over Addlebury!"

Addlebury was Wudgi's great rival in the area. Only fifteen miles distant, Addlebury boasted all the government agencies, a proper supermarket – that great new invention of the 1950's - and two Hotels. Bill Outstanding nodded in appreciation of the point.

"Er...costs, Monsewer. What sort of costs are we looking at? That's going to have to be our primary consideration."

"I vill scout out ze land, as you say, and let you know. I'se tink it vill not be 'over ze top'."

There the matter rested for the next three days. Enrico was duly noted up and down the main street, taking measurements with a slide rule, and pacing backwards and forwards across the road. Then he was down at the bridge over the Wudgi Creek, mapping out a turning circle for the tram.

What he had omitted to inform the luminaries of Wudgi, was that almost every city in the civilized world was at that moment either scrapping their tram systems, or had already done so. The prevailing view was that they were outdated and inconvenient, and the rails took up valuable roadway, which could be utilized by both trolley buses and private cars.

Town Clerk Jeremiah Pickandle returned to find a fait accompli had been effected in his absence, and he wasn't happy about it.

"The council had no right to push this through without the Town Clerk's input," he complained. "The whole thing's a mare's nest. What do we want with a tram?"

"The decision has been made, Pickandle, by a vote of the council. As a paid employee of the council, I would expect you to do all in your power to expedite the inauguration of this great step forward," said Mayor Outstanding, haughtily.

"I don't like it, and I don't like this Enrico character either. What references have you sighted? How do we know he can do the job?"

"Have a little faith, Pickandle. We are accomplishing great things here in Wudgi Crossing. Be part of it, man, or give good reason why the rate-payers should continue to employ someone who doesn't have their best interests at heart."

Pickandle went off mumbling about he'd show them who had the best interests of the rate-payers at heart, and it wasn't the elected council yobbo's, who were a pack of amateurs anyway, and he didn't believe in progress for its own sake especially in a one horse town like Wudgi Crossing that was going nowhere faster than speeding bullet and he should have got the job at Addlebury only that Barry McWaters beat him to it which only goes to show that it's not what you know but who, because Barry was the son of the garbage collector who'd won the contract for the past seventeen years because his uncle was the Mayor's wife's brother and Addlebury was full of McWaters, and the name kept popping up on every contract the council put out for some strange reason, and so on for another twenty minutes locked in the privacy of his office.

So it was that before even the first rail was set in cement, the tram project had won itself a dire enemy, and Pickandle wasted no time in enlisting on his side the ganger in charge of the works depot – Freddy Steamshovel. The two had conspired together in the past in the old 'employees' versus 'elected members' on the council, and the honours had often gone to the employees. This time, both Pickandle and Steamshovel were determined to win out.

Enrico, in the meantime, came up with an estimate that made the scheme quite attainable. He had managed to tee up a double-decker tram from the old Birmingham, England, network, and this came with two extra trams in bits, for spare parts. The rail was not a problem, as this could be brought in from South Africa at a discount as ship's ballast. Having got the go-ahead, it was only a matter of six weeks before the tram arrived, by which time the rail was already there, and being installed.

The overhead cabling came in from Rio de Janeiro, and the main street of Wudgi was soon a hive of activity as thirteen workmen – more than anyone had ever seen actually working in Wudgi at any one time – put up posts to support the electrified grid, attached stays to verandahs and buildings, and ran this network down the hill towards the bridge. The rail was laid as a 3 foot 6 inch gauge, and the day came when the tram, on a low-loader, trundled slowly over the bridge and was hauled up the hill to be deposited onto the rails at the new terminus, outside Amos Feeble's Grocery Store.

It was a great day for Wudgi, and anyone who was anyone was there to celebrate the new era., including two or three inconspicuous 'observers' from Addlebury, each of them named McWaters. Also on the sidelines, looking grim and determined, were both Pickandle and Steamshovel. They had watched the installations going ahead with dismay, but with no plan as yet to counter the general acceptance of the Wudgi Tram.

Once on the rails, the tram sat there resplendent in its Birmingham livery of navy blue and cream.

The Mayor gave his acceptance speech, and indicated that the tram would be repainted in new colours, "…in keeping with the dignity of Wudgi Crossing," he said. "Probably purple with pink hoops."

Then the good people of Wudgi were allowed to inspect the tram, board it, sit on its seats and climb the stairs at the back to admire the upper level. It was certainly not immaculate, but it was an object of wonder for the good Wudgi folk, most of whom had never seen a tram before.

"Ooooh, Edna," said one fat lady. "Those Birmingham folk must have skinny bums, because I can't get all of mine on the seat."

"And they must have short legs, 'cos mine are jammed up against the back of the seat in front," said Edna, who was six foot nine.

But apart from these few complaints, everyone got off feeling very proud and satisfied with the new acquisition.

The power had not been connected at that stage, so there was no question of going for a tour down the hill. That would come later. The Mayor assured everyone that their first ride would be free, but that after that, the fare would be three'pence going up the hill, and tuppence going down. So for less than a zac you could go both ways.

"What about children," yelled out a mother of five.

"Yeah, what about the kids," reiterated another.

After struggling with the mental arithmetic required for such an equation, and looking around him for help, but finding none, the Mayor replied: "Errrr....well, say under twelve, tuppence going up the hill, and a penny ha'penny going down. Over twelve, full fare." Then he got off his rostrum as quickly as possible to avoid any further speculation.

Everything had gone swimmingly to this point, so the first mishap was entirely unexpected. Two days later power was applied to the overhead grid, and the tram set up a steady hum as its motors turned. But there was also a strange buzzing sound coming from the verandah outside Madame Le Strange's hairdressing shop. As people walked underneath it, their hair suddenly and unaccountably stood up on end.

"Here, this is a bit much," said Mrs. Hennessy, trying to control her bouffant hairdo, which had cost her eight pounds at Addlebury. "I've heard of drumming up business, but this is ridiculous."

Madame Le Strange shortly found herself the subject of more prolonged abuse.

"Look what you've done to my hair," said Anne Marie Fitzwaller, looking like a golliwog on a bad hair day. Her curls floated incongruously a foot above her head. Ladies leaving the shop immaculately permed and blow-dried were instantly transformed as they stepped into the street, to howls of laughter, and indignation from the victims. It was a mystery, and Madame Le Strange was as mystified as everyone else.

Eric Beagle, an innocuous insurance agent with a hair lip and a hair-piece, walked past at five to two, and suddenly reached for his scalp as he felt a rush of cold air hit his cranium. Looking up, he could see his hairpiece stuck to the underside of the corrugated iron verandah roof, totally out of reach.

At two p.m. precisely, Beryl Huntingdon-Foxhandler arrived for her appointment, her pet poodle in tow. She secured the poodle to a verandah post, felt her hair rise magically into the air, and made a dash for the entrance to Madame Le Strange's. Once inside, the effect began to subside, but outside, Pookie the Poodle had decided to relieve itself against the rainwater pipe, which itself was attached to the verandah post the pooch was secured to. It merely lifted its leg, and then:

"Well, I've never seen anything like it," said Anne Marie, later. "Suddenly this fluffy little dog just burst into flames."

"It gave one big squirt, burst into flames and then exploded all over me," said Henry McWalters, back in Addlebury. "I think we'd better give the tram a miss; let Wudgi have all the hassle."

Bits of Pookie were plastered over the window of the hairdressers, the underside of the verandah, and the side of the tram parked opposite. Town Clerk Pickandle socked one fist into the palm of the other in delight. At last, something to get his teeth into! He strode over to the Mayor, who was having an intense discussion with Enrico.

"I hope you saw that, Outstanding. You've blown up a poodle. I knew this blasted tram was a mare's nest."

"Just a teething problem, Blithering. There's bound to be a few hiccups."

"Eeeet looks as if ze verandah his helectrified," said Enrico, frowning. "Zey must have shorted out ze high tension."

Sure enough, one of the workmen had improperly secured a live cable to Madame Le

Strange's verandah roof, and 22,000 volts was setting up a static charge under the verandah strong enough to raise hair. Once earthed, however, it was like being hit by a bolt of lightning.

Ignoring the implications of this, Enrico took his place at the controls, and with the Mayor beside him, the tram moved off graciously along the main street. Keeping to a steady fifteen miles an hour, the tram moved along with a slight hissing sound, and a low rumble on the line. Faultlessly it dipped to move down the hill, and it maintained a slow, average speed until it got to the roundabout at the bottom by the bridge, where it executed a perfect arc and headed back the way it had come.

The hill at Wudgi is fairly steep at one point, and it was there that the tram exhibited a tendency to spin the driving wheels, sending out a shower of sparks from beneath the chassis. But the grip held, and the tram regained the flat to the sound of cheers from the local population, and swept back to its terminus in a proud passage at twenty two miles an hour.

As the width of the road outside the grocers did not allow of a turning circle, Enrico had acquired a mechanical turntable, which he had converted to be driven by the same power source as the tram.

Driving the tram onto the turntable, the platform began to move ponderously around, facing the tram back in the opposite direction. Enrico then drove off the turntable and parked outside Madame Le Strange's.

"Perfect," smiled the Mayor.

"Stuff it!" growled Pickandle, watching from a distance. "However," he turned to Steamshovel; "That has given me an idea. Tonight we act!"

The rest of the afternoon was taken up with giving townsfolk free rides down the hill and back up again, with the newly appointed driver Samuel Griptite at the controls. Still a prey to solecisms; nevertheless, the Mayor had decided that Griptite was well enough known by now to be disregarded when he came out with inappropriate statements. He was willing to give him a chance.

"All aboard who's getting aboard" soon became 'Older beards, whose betting a bone?' 'Get your tickets out,' became 'mind your biscuits', and 'all change at the terminal' became 'get off anybody at Tommy Null's.' But nobody minded.

That night, Pickandle and Steamshovel waited until the street was deserted, then hurried off down the main street, keeping in the shadows, and carrying a large tin. Just at the point where the hill became steepest, Steamshovel dashed out of the shadows and deposited large gobs of some glutinous red substance out of the tin, and onto each rail. He repeated this at intervals further down the lines, unaware that he was being observed by Abigail Woolgathering, from the front window of her cottage.

"I had a look, later, when they had both disappeared," she told the Mayor. "I put my hands in it, and it was grease," she reported. "So I went in and got a couple of tea-towels, came out and scooped up what I could. They wanted the tram to crash, or something. I couldn't believe it."

Mayor Outstanding told her to keep it under her hat, that he would have to catch them in the act before he could do anything about it. He proposed that they set a trap the following day, and see if they tried it again.

The next day, Pickandle and Steamshovel were lounging against the wall of the Wudgi Arms Hotel when the tram made its first run down the hill at 8.30 a.m. As it dipped to go down, the two of them rushed out, peering to see what would happen when it hit the grease.

"Aah, Pickandle – and err... Steamshovel! You're out early this morning," said the Mayor, as he poked his head out of the door of the pub. "What brings you out this fine morning.?"

Pickandle had the grace to look guilty, and mumbled something about 'just checking on the tram.' Steamshovel said nothing, just looked abashed.

"It's good to see that we have some support from you at last," smiled the Mayor, and withdrew back inside the Wudgi Arms.

"What's he up to?" said Pickandle. "Someone's tipped him off. He's never up at this hour of the morning."

By this time the tram had arrived at the bottom of the hill without mishap, and was turning around for the return journey.

"All binge for the Wudgi caramel," Griptite sang out to an old swaggy, who was clutching the side of the bridge in fright. He'd never seen a tram before, and thought he must have the D.T.'s. Looking around, the swaggy tried to see if there was anyone else in the area, otherwise the driver must have been talking to him!"

"Get your busket here," said Griptite, fixing the swaggy with a persuasive stare. "Come and join the travelogue – only three ponces up to the germinal."

The swaggy ducked under the bridge and hid, hoping that when he looked out again the tram would be gone. It was. He fell back in a half swoon, and thought – 'I'll never drink shoe polish again, so 'elp me!'

On the way back up the hill, Griptite thought he felt a lack of traction, and the tram laboured somewhat to get over the crest. This would remain the pattern for the rest of the morning, until the tram, fully loaded with shoppers at twelve thirty, began its lunchtime descent.

Sitting disguised in the rear were two hairy looking women, each with a can of motor oil between their feet. As the tram descended they managed to hang out of the rear entrance on each side, and trickle a steady stream of oil onto the tracks the tram had just passed along. The oil followed its inclination, and began to flow steadily along the groove of each line in the tram's wake. At the bottom, the two got off, and made for the bridge.

"Well, well, well…. Aren't these two quite the ugliest women you've ever seen," bellowed Mayor Outstanding, as he appeared from his hiding place, under the bridge. Beside him was the Reverend

Holysmock, and behind them were two other councillors and Abigail Woolgathering.

"Well, Pickandle, are you an idiot or what? And you Steamshovel – what were you thinking of? Never mind; you're both fired. You can pick up your pay on Friday."

By this time the tram had made its turn, and was heading back up the hill with half of its passengers still aboard, most of them still experiencing the novelty of a tram ride. Three quarters of the way up the hill, the tram met the descending run of oil, and began to spin its wheels. Unable to get any traction at all this time, the tram slowed to a stop, then began to slide backwards.

The Mayor's party were walking up the hill when the tram hurtled past them, going in reverse. The momentum was such that when it hit the turning circle at the bottom, it jumped the tracks and headed off into the bush. As it disappeared amongst the trees there was a loud wailing set up amongst the passengers, above which the voice of Griptite could be heard: "Hang on to your boodles – don't picnic everybody! Keep your beds and hang on to the bracelets!" His white face was the last thing the Mayor's party saw as he was whisked in reverse towards the Wudgi swamp.

It is not generally known, but just at that moment, Sir Barley de Water Devereaux was donning a wet suit at the edge of the swamp, where he intended hunting the giant bilbeys rumoured to be located in the mangroves. He had just spotted a giant newt, when through the trees came a huge tram, travelling at speed, full of screaming people. Sir Barley was so taken aback that his jaw dropped, and he just turned to stare at it, quite forgetting that on the odd occasion when one meets a hurtling tram in the deep woods, one must necessarily jump out of the way. The tram ran straight over the top of him, depositing him under twenty five tons of steel and coachwork at the bottom of the Wudgi swamp.

As it settled, ladies were popping out of windows and doors and coming up covered in fish eggs and weeds. (At least, I think they were fish eggs). Those on the upper deck were relatively untouched. When help came in the form of a long plank balanced between the upper deck and the solid edge of the swamp, only three ladies managed to fall off the plank before getting safely ashore.

And that was the end of the Wudgi Tram. A very young Angus McSoufflé came along one day and spotted the top deck of the tram still sitting above the swamp, and paid the council $10 a year to lease it. He then turned it into a fish and chip shop, and thus began his long career as a restaurateur.

Enrico never got paid. He seems to blame the Mayor, though it was really a collective decision. However, regular as clockwork, once a month, an invoice arrives at the Wudgi council offices with Enrico's letterhead at the top. Each time the same amount is claimed, for goods and services, though the councillors maintain that the bill is not addressed to them anyway, so why should they pay it?

In the middle of the invoice, stamped in large letters, in red ink, is the message 'Bill Outstanding'; and so it gets passed on to Bill, every month. Even if he could, Bill has no intentions of paying it, now or at any time. He's just hoping that Enrico shows up one day, so that he can let him know, in no uncertain terms, what he thinks about having his municipal career ruined. To that end he keeps a two-foot piece of tramline just behind his front door.

McSoufflé and the Flying Saucer

When the creek starts flowing at Wudgi Crossing, the locals know that winter is finally there, and they put up the shutters and check the guttering and roof for leaks, lay in a stock of firewood, and hibernate for the winter. That's all there is to it, usually. Nothing happens at Wudgi during the winter; in fact for the younger folks, it gets plain boring.

Occasionally, after a heavy fall of rain, the creek will run a 'banker', and the water will overflow onto the road down by the bridge, even getting up to two feet deep at such times, and effectively cutting Wudgi off from the rest of the civilized world. The West Coast Bus ceases to run at such times, and the locals are forced to do their major shop at Fred Feeble's store, instead of making the fortnightly trip up to Addlebury, to the supermarket there. Thus it was in the winter of '99.

The creek was running a banker, and the rain continued to fall steadily, causing the waters to rise to three feet, then four, spill across through the woods and into the swamp. It even submerged what was left showing of the old Wudgi Tram, which had been deserted for years by this time, though the upper deck had still carried a few signs from the days of Angus McSoufflé's days of fish and chips. He'd progressed since then to his own restaurant, and was getting a bit long in the tooth by this. But he was a cunning old fox was Angus, and had been known to serve up Batwing soup, Bilbey steaks with Newt sauce, not to mention the Rustik Flok series of Burgers and soft drinks that had almost ruined him. He was an opportunist of the first water, and always on the lookout for a new gimmick to put bums on seats.

Wintertime was not a good time for the restaurant. People sat home and watched videos, or huddled in front of wood fires to stay warm. They rarely ventured out once it got dark, so often the restaurant remained empty, burning up money by wasting electricity on the lights and on the grill plate. At such times McSoufflé would stand outside his front door, even in the rain, cursing his luck and the good folk of Wudgi for not being more adventurous.

The only people who seemed to venture out were those who made their living from the land, the local farmers. No matter what the weather, they had a variety of tasks, which had to be repeated every day, and they were out in all weathers. Col

Springett was down in his bottom paddock trying to move a sick cow, late one afternoon, and he wasn't having much luck. The old girl was down on her haunches, and couldn't get up. Gradually it got dark, and then began to rain once more, and Col cursed as he realized he would have to leg it back to the farmhouse, because his son had taken the tractor an hour before so he could give it a service. It was a good mile back to the farmhouse, and Col was already soaked to the skin. So he set off.

He had just arrived at the paddock gate, when an eery pink glow began to make its presence felt on the other side of the hedge. Puzzled, Col climbed over the gate and walked around to see where this light was coming from. There was a tree break, with thick bushes in the corner of the next paddock, and the glow was filtering through the trees. Whatever it was, it was behind the bushes.

Not one to panic, Col strode across, determined to find out what was giving off that unearthly light. Whoever it was, they were on his land, and he didn't like trespassers. He was just working himself up to give someone a bollocking, when he rounded the bushes and saw the flying saucer for the first time.

"No bloody joke, Bazza," he relayed later in the Wudgi Arms. "I tell you if I hadn't seen it with me own eyes, I would never have believed it. A bloody flying saucer! True! It was round and shaped like a dish – about twenty feet across. And it had little windows all around the rim, and that's where this pink light was coming from."

"What did you do, Col?" someone shouted out.

"What do yer think I did? I bloody took off, mate. Phar Lap had nothin' on me, I tell yer! I was across that paddock and – you know that wire fence on the other side; how high do you reckon that is?"

"Four foot," said the same voice.

"Well I sailed over that with one bloody great leap, and I don't reckon I stopped 'til I got back to the farmhouse."

"…where he changed his jocks," some wit remarked, and the pub crowd broke up, laughing.

"You can bloody joke, mate. Wait 'til you come across it. We'll see how brave you are."

"Ah, come on, Col. You were just mistaken, that's all. It was raining, and it was dark, it was probably some kids playing silly buggers with a lantern. You know what they're like around here."

"It was a flying saucer I tell yer. I know what I

saw!"

With little else to talk about, it was around the town the following day, how Col Springett had seen a flying saucer in his side paddock. The topic even came up at the council meeting.

"Do you think he's gone a bit loopy?" said Mrs Blithe-Brown, addressing the chamber in general.

"It fair gives me the creeps," said Mrs. Harkpea, the Progress Association's long-suffering secretary. "What if it is – a flying saucer, that is – and aliens have come to collect specimens of earthlings?"

"You've been watching too many science fiction movies, Sarah," growled 'Rough' Red, the Mayor. "If it is aliens, why would they come to Wudgi of all places? Why not Sydney or Melbourne? They'd get a better selection there."

"That's just it," said Mrs. Harkpea. "Maybe they just do this sort of thing on the quiet. Out here they can get away before anyone knows anything about it."

"Well, aliens or no aliens, if they come into our town, then they'll have to obey the local ordinances – it's in the local government act," said Bill Beakheaper, the Town Clerk. "They'll be covered by the same bye-laws as everyone else. If they show up again, we'd better get a delegation together to go and meet them, and give them a rundown on the law." Bill was a stickler for protocol.

"Oh yes, and what law is that may I ask?" said Mrs. Blithe-Brown, adopting her superior tone.

"That you can't go round kidnapping people. It's not politically correct," growled the Mayor. "Bill's right, it's up to us to act as the go-betweens. We're cut off from Addlebury – and everywhere else at the moment. So I'll want volunteers for the delegation."

There was a sudden silence in the chamber, then a hurried gathering of bags and briefcases. Before a single hand went up, the Mayor and Town Clerk had the room to themselves.

The following day, it rained. It not only rained, it poured! At four o'clock in the afternoon, Cora Littledove came pedaling her three-wheeler up over the crest of the hill in the main street, her legs going like pistons. As she approached the row of businesses at the top, she let out a blood-curdling scream, which had the shopkeepers rushing out of their front doors to see what the commotion was about. Some twenty yards behind her, and closing fast, was a flying saucer.

It was just as Col Springett had described it. It was circular, with porthole type windows all around, and it floated above the ground emitting a muffled roar as it swept past. A strange, pink light emanated from the portholes.

"Don't let them get me," Cora screamed. "I haven't done anything to them. They've chased me up from the bridge."

Fred Feeble dashed out and dragged her off her bike and into his shop. She was too good a customer to lose to little green men. Everyone else dashed inside and slammed and locked their doors, then peered out into the murk. The saucer came to a halt, then spun slowly around on its axis, before heading off down the street again and disappearing over the crest of the hill.

"Well, I never," said Mrs. Blithe-Brown, who had been picking up a packet of soap powder in Fred's shop. "Col was right. They've come to get us, Fred. They're just giving us a warning – resistance is useless." Her voice gradually rose, an octave at a time, as Mrs. Blithe-Brown gave in, for the first time in her life, to hysteria. "They do medical experiments, don't they Fred? They cut people up to find out how they work. They don't even use anaesthetics, Fred. They hypnotise you, and you can't move a muscle. Then they start to cut you open with big curved knives and laser beams, slowly, and all your insides fall out all over the floor – I've seen it, Fred, I've seen it on the movies."

By this time she had Fred by the throat, and had him pinned against the wall by the fresh fish display case. He was trying to catch his breath to answer her, so he could calm her down, but she was a woman of considerable strength, and in her delerium she was squeezing him tighter and tighter until his throat closed over. At that point he slapped her twice around the head with a large schnapper that he managed to fish out of the display case, and she staggered back in confusion.

"Now look what you made me do," he gasped, indicating the schnapper lying on the floor. "You're going to have to buy that. I can't sell it to anyone else."

Elsewhere, both men and women were dissolving into hysterics, and when it was discovered that the phone lines into the town were down, the panic really set in.

"We're isolated, cut off," sobbed Sarah Harkpea to her husband, Des, who had been asleep on the sofa while the whole saucer thing was going on. "They wouldn't listen to me at the council, made fun of poor Col Springett – but he was right. He did see it. And now we've all seen it. I can't even phone my mother," she sobbed. "Do you think it'll be painful when…"

"When what, dear?" said Des Harkpea, peering over his copy of the Wudgi Chronicle. He had just sat down, packed his pipe, and was enjoying his easy chair and the paper for the first time that day.

"When they come to take us away."

Des looked bewildered, and somewhat irritated. He never listened to his wife unless he absolutely had to, and now here she was, destroying his concentration by asking him questions.

"Who? Who come to get us, dear?" He pulled a face.

"These little green men, Des. The ones in the flying saucer! Haven't you been listening to me?"

Des looked at her strangely, as if he was trying to make up his mind about something. "I think it's time you resigned from that committee, Sarah. You've been under a lot of pressure, and if you're not careful you might… well… you might end up with a nervous breakdown."

"But what about the little green men?" she

shouted at him.

"Well, they might have a nervous breakdown too," he replied, soothingly, and went back to his paper.

There was nothing short of panic in the streets by this time. Doors were locked and barred all through the town, and the publican of the Wudgi Arms Hotel scrutinised everyone minutely before he allowed them through the door.

"Who is it?" he yelled out from behind the closed door.

"Who the bloody 'ell do you think it is," replied Jim Mopandle, annoyed at this halt in his passage.

"This isn't a guessing game, mate. Who is it, and how can you prove it?"

"It's Jim Mopandle, and I've been coming to this pub, every afternoon, at this time, for over thirty years – as you well know."

"How do I know that? You might *look* like Jim Mopandle, and you might *sound* like Jim Mopandle, but you might have been taken over by an alien, too."

"If you don't open that bloody door, Barry Pullever, and get me a drink, you'll be picking splinters out of your nose for a fortnight."

Bazza let him in, then locked the door behind

him.

"Now *that's* Jim Mopandle," he said to his other patrons, as he walked back behind the bar. "No alien would be that bloody rude!"

That night, in the bar of the Wudgi Arms, a meeting was held to discuss the situation.

"Everyone will have to arm themselves," said Merv Malachi. "I've got an old shotgun, and most of you have got a .22 or something. We'll have to set up a watch on the main street. If it comes back again, we'll let it have it."

"My old 12 gauge double barrel will make a mess of it," said Col Springett. "It won't be flying off to new planets after that's finished with it."

"Hear hear," said the rest of the crew through their schooners.

"Ern Pigswill has got a .303. Who's going to volunteer to go out there and bring him in?" Everyone looked at each other, and shook their heads. Maybe they could get by on the 12 gauge, and a couple of .22's.

That night, five men took up their positions at the top of the main street, on either side of the road. There was a slight drizzle, and the night was cold, so they huddled back into the buildings and hid in the shadows. A dim moonlight glinted off the barrels of their rifles.

At 8.30 p.m. someone sighted a glow down over the crest of the hill, and shortly a saucer shaped object came gliding up the road towards them, glowing pink. It gave out a dull roar as it approached, and the guardians of Wudgi called out to each other.

"Don't fire until you see the pink of its windows," whispered Col Springett. "Wait 'til I give the okay."

The clatter of boots receding up the road told Col that at least three of his fellow defenders had lost their nerve, and were headed for the hills. That left him and Merv Malachi, and Merv had dropped his shotgun in a puddle and soiled himself. He stood there now in a blue funk, his hands shaking, unable to move a muscle.

"It's no good, Col. The bastards have got ray guns and lasers. They'll just make our bullets turn around in midair, and we'll end up in the stewpot."

"For Chrisesake, don't go soft on me now, Merv," said Col, who was beginning to have serious doubts of his own.

"Maybe we should parley with them, then if they want some hostages they can take that old cow Blithe-Brown, or someone on the council. Oh shit, Col. It's gonna stop!"

Sure enough, the flying saucer glided up in front of them, slowing all the while, then stopped, not twenty yards away. The roaring sound diminished, and the saucer slowly sank down onto the road.

"What are you gonna do, Col?" said Merv, totally un-nerved by now. Col grimaced, then made up his mind.

"I'm gonna get me a little green man," he said, savagely, and brought his shotgun up to his shoulder.

Just then there was a sound that seemed very familiar. From somewhere in the saucer a speaker blared, and it was some moments before the two recognized the tune as 'Greensleeves'. Then a cone on the top of the saucer began to rise, and underneath it, the figure of a man.

"Anyone for soup, gentlemen," said Angus McSoufflé, in his best entrepreneurial tone. Noting their shocked faces, he went on – "or coffee, tea, hot dogs; how about a nice hot dog with chilli sauce, Col. You look frozen!"

It was a good two minutes before either Col Springett or Merv Malachi could speak. When they did it was in concert with dragging McSoufflé out of the saucer by the scruff of his neck.

"You bastard, McSoufflé, it was you all the time. We thought it was a bloody flying saucer. If it's not a flying saucer, what is it?"

"Hang on, hang on boys. No need to get rough. It's the latest in fast food delivery; a hovercraft. I got this one second-hand, and thought I'd service the main street after dark, when everyone else is closed. The restaurant is pretty quiet at this time of year."

"So what the hell were you doing yesterday, coming up the main street, then taking off again without letting everyone know what it was?"

Angus looked at them in his superior way, and adjusted his jacket.

"Marketing, boys, just marketing! Whetting people's appetites by just being a bit mysterious. Plus, of course, I was getting used to using the controls. It's not as easy as it looks."

Col looked at him, his eyes glaring.

"You bloody nearly gave Cora Littledove a heart attack! You've had the whole town up in arms. You'll be lucky if you sell a sausage after this!"

Angus was hauled before the council and severely admonished for creating such a panic in the town. Then, as an added punishment, Mrs. Blithe-Brown suggested that he only be licensed to operate at the Wudgi swamp, next to the old tram. She had a vivid memory of being slapped with a wet fish, and was determined that McSoufflé would pay for that, one way or the other.

Thus it was that McSoufflé's flying saucer was banned from the town limits, and he never got to dispense hot food to the local populace. It sits today around the back of the restaurant, surrounded by weeds, an expensive reminder to Angus that, sometimes, you could be just a little bit too clever for yourself.

There is an appendix to this story. I wasn't going to include it, because I know you'll never believe me anyway, so there's not really much point. But about six weeks after Angus had been banished from operating in the near environs of Wudgi township, a flying saucer came zooming up the main street of Wudgi Crossing, sat on the old tram turntable, and started it spinning at high speed. 'Rough' Red was first on the scene, and he wasn't going to stand for any nonsense.

"McSoufflé," he yelled. "Get that bloody thing off the turntable, and stop pissing about! If you don't obey the council edict, we'll have your restaurant licence!"

The flying saucer took no notice of the Mayor, but continued to spin as if it were on a merry-go-round. The Town Clerk saw the Mayor being ignored, and came running over as reinforcements. He approached the saucer to within touching distance, and yelled out: "McSoufflé, we know you're in there. If you don't stop, I'll call out the Fire Chief, and have you hosed down."

Nothing anyone said seemed to have any effect. The old turntable was setting up a peculiar whine by this time. It wasn't designed to spin at high speed. Then suddenly it stopped, waited a few moments and began to spin in the opposite direction.

"Now that's bloody enough," said Bill Beakheaper. "I will not put up with you undermining the dignity of the Mayor's high office. I order you to stop!"

Just at that moment, Angus McSoufflé wandered out of Fred Feeble's shop, where he had been purchasing cleaning materials for the restaurant.

"Did I hear my name being used in vain," he exclaimed. Then he spotted the flying saucer.

145

"Well, I say – a new model! Very impressive!"

Beakheaper turned and gaped at him.

"What are you doing there, McSoufflé, when you're in there?" He indicated the saucer.

"It seems to be self-evident, old man," said McSoufflé, amiably. "I'm out here, so you can't blame *me* this time. Whose little joke is this, then?" He nodded towards the saucer.

Beakheaper gingerly reached out and touched the spinning rim of the saucer, and suddenly all hell let loose. A siren started up from somewhere inside the saucer, and it stopped spinning on the spot. It then made a humming noise, and Beakheaper lit up in a pale blue light, and floated up off the ground several feet. Everyone else backed off.

"Hey – hey-ay-ay-ay!" yelled the Town Clerk. "Let me down. I thought it was McSoufflé, oh god, what's happening?"

"Something began to drip out from Beakheaper's trouser legs, and whatever it was, it wasn't very nice."

"Look, he's melting," yelled some woman in horror.

"No he's not, he's crapping himself," said Emmanuel Belchfire, who had just turned up with his fire engine. "That's okay, we can hose him down afterwards."

But contrary to the Fire Chief's explanation, Beakheaper was not suffering from a sudden fit of the runs. That became obvious when his heart suddenly burst out of his chest, and hung there in the air, tumbling first this way and then that as if an invisible hand was inspecting it. Beakheaper seemed to have lost interest at this point, as he ceased to struggle, and just hung there. One after another his organs suddenly popped out of his body, and underwent the same inspection process. By this time, however, everyone who could run was running, and old Elias Carbunkle was taking his wheelchair down the hill at a speed in excess of thirty miles an hour.

The Town Clerk's body continued to hang in the air as his brain slid slowly out of his left nostril, and his teeth popped out and danced a jig in the air, twisting and turning every which way. Finally, all the organs having been inspected, they fell with a mighty splat onto the bitumen, followed by the empty carcass of Wudgi's Town Clerk. Then a bolt of what seemed like lightning shot out from the saucer, and cremated the remains on the spot. They were still blazing with an intense white light when the flying saucer shot off down the street again, this time at a height of about twenty feet. Hovercraft can't do that!

It wasn't over yet, however. Those few observers who were left, hiding in ditches and in the corners of buildings, saw an unearthly glow emanate from the middle of the road as the saucer passed overhead. It was the steel tramlines that no one had seen for fifty years, glowing from underneath the tarmac in response to some energy derived from the saucer. Perhaps it was the magnetic field they could see – perhaps that was what had brought the saucer to Wudgi, to investigate an ancient magnetic field, thought to be a landing ground for flying saucers? Who knows! But whatever it had learned from an inspection of the Town Clerk, the beings in the saucer must have rifled his brain for memories as well, otherwise there would be no sense to what happened next.

Shooting down over the crest of the hill, the saucer headed into the woods and towards the Wudgi swamp. Not ten minutes later, an apparition trundled out of the woods that god-fearing folk thought must have been the work of the devil. For there, trundling along, dripping weed and emptying water from its decks, and covered in a green mosslike fungus, was the Wudgi Tram.

Over the top of it hovered the flying saucer, and it progressed inexorably up the street towards the old terminus, rumbling over the tarmac where the rails were buried, and dripping sludge like an evil omen from the distant past. The saucer set the Tram down on the old turntable, then with a dipping movement is if it were tipping its hat at Wudgi, it zoomed off into the stratosphere, and was never seen again.

I told you, you wouldn't believe me! (Oh, all right, I made up the bit about the tram – Okay?)

A Gruesome Interlude

On the hill where Mick McGurk parked his tent in 1862 stands a sombre looking building that throws long shadows through the afternoon, bringing a sense of doom and gloom to this part of the old town of Wudgi Crossing. This is the *Wudgi Sanatorium for the Criminally Insane.* It's built in old red brick, in the vague style of a 19th century Manchester Cotton Warehouse. The only difference is that the architect, being a bit of a medievalist at heart, threw in turrets, battlements and a portcullis.

The locals have long since learned to ignore its existence, or, if forced to mention it in passing describe it as the 'Wusky', which is as close as they can get to its initials. It sits pensively on the corner of Damnation Street, and Rollicking Row, the latter named for the large number of sailors who were confined within its towers in the days of sailing ships. In those days you only had to be drunk to get locked up.

Dark and forbidding, the architect wasn't content to contain the inhabitants with ten-foot iron gates, (over which a sign proclaimed – *'Abandon your Wife when you enter these Portals'* –

presumably to discourage whole families from moving in). No – he wanted to scare off the local populace as well, put a dent in their curiosity. So he placed gargoyles strategically along the eves, evil-looking monsters that streamed water out into the street whenever it rained. The gargoyles each side of the gates also streamed water during times of drought, but only if you were foolish enough to push the brass bell. No one has been silly enough to push that bell for fifty years.

Behind the gates there is a portcullis, permanently raised these days, though in the event of an emergency I am assured that it still works. Pull out a pin and it comes hurtling down at fifty miles an hour, as a laundry van found out to its cost in 1927. The front half of the van still lies in a ditch at the bottom of the hill, while the rear end languishes in the shadow of a turret, and is now used as a dog kennel. There is still no word on the driver.

There is one other entrance, the tradesman's at the back. Here there are no iron gates, just a wooden door leading directly into the kitchen, where a 27 stone cook once threatened everyone entering with a plate of tripe and onions. If you didn't tuck in straight away, she hit you with an enormous wooden spoon and made you stand in the corner for the rest of the afternoon.

One memorable day she had the milkman, the plumber, two apprentices and the local constable all bailed up behind the refrigerator, and wouldn't let them go until after the pub had closed at six o'clock. (Remember 6 o'clock closing?) She was duly charged with illegally detaining them against their will, etc., before it was realized that she was an inmate anyway, and five sandwiches short of a picnic. The charges were dropped.

As asylums go, it was one of the best of its kind – in 1888. Of course times changed, and the lunatic of more modern times expected just a little more than a padded cell, a small cot, and a bucket in the corner which had to be emptied every morning. They also resented being shackled in the bath-house for some reason, arguing that they couldn't get their clothes off.

Maude Sadismo, the senior wardress, wouldn't take any of that nonsense, though. A massive woman, six foot three in her knickerbockers, it was said that she could pick up any man by his scrotum and swing him around her head, before aiming him at a full bath, and launching him like a javelin.

"Don't use that old excuse with me, my lad," she would say. "Yer a dirty bugger that doesn't want to wash. Make sure you dry those irons when you get out; we wouldn't want them to get all rusty, would we?"

"It's a good job these baths are only two foot deep, isn't it? Any deeper and we'd go straight to the bottom," said Admiral Lord Nelson one day, coming up and spluttering for breath.

"Any lip out of you, and I'll fix your other eye for you," said Maude. She was not exactly sympathetic to the plight of her charges.

Maude had been in charge for over twenty years, and she often said that she'd still come to work, even if they didn't pay her. She enjoyed the sense of power it gave her over others less fortunate than herself. Unlucky in love, she had found her vocation in torturing the already demented. After all, they couldn't complain, could they? And if they did, who would listen to them?

Up in one of the turrets she had a secret little room that held electrical apparatus, a couch with straps and buckles, and some plug-in boxes with switches and rheostats and voltage regulators – all sorts of goodies. If an inmate misbehaved she would give them one warning.

"Once more, and it's the brain-trainer for you," she would say. And they all knew exactly what that meant, because she made sure that each new inmate was ushered up there within the first week of arrival for a quick flush out of the memory banks. Fifty volts used to work a treat.

As she strapped them into the apparatus, and attached the electrodes to their heads, she would lean over them, gloating, and say - "I'm your worst nightmare, come true!"

If you took a roll call at the Wusky, for any time over the past century, you would be able to make up quite a catalogue of famous names. Three Nelsons, five Napoleon Buonaparte's, Anne Boleyn, a couple of Cleopatra's, no less than eight Julius Caesar's, two Mark Anthony's, and on a more mundane note; three roly poly puddings, a jam tart, a swiss roll, and a bowl of sago. That's not to mention the sticks of rhubarb, two carrots – one blue, one green; and the lemon meringue pies of which there have been dozens.

In the more mechanical fixations, the Wusky could number a Model T Ford, a mincing machine, a cherry picker, two bulldozers, a double-decker bus and a spinning top. It was bedlam when they all started up together.

In these more enlightened times, the number of inmates have dwindled to a mere handful compared to the peak of 345 in 1968. At last count there were only 27 inmates in the WUSKY, and thirteen staff members to look after them. But if there is a paucity of numbers, at least the quality is still there.

Chief of their number is a retired High Court Judge, one Sir Humphrey Aberfoyle Stubbit, who is now in his 91st year, and looking fit enough to make his century. Sir Humphrey holds his court each week in the annex off the dining room, and makes arbitrary judgements on both inmates and kitchen staff; not that anyone takes much notice. His chief opponent in these hearings is Napoleon, also known as Rusty Drinkwater to the staff, though he refuses to answer to any title other than Emperor. Their courtroom battles, over the past twelve months or so, have been magnificent. The score stands at Napoleon 23, Judge Stubbit 35, for those who are counting.

Skulking in the wings at these battles is a pastry-cook who murdered his mother and her new boyfriend by feeding them quiche, sprinkled with Ratsak. Russell Avabite is his name, though he has recently been introducing himself to the Sanatorium cat as 'The Duke of Wellington'. Every time Napoleon wins a point, he yells out "Waterloo" at the top of his voice, then skulks down behind a pillar as Napoleon stomps wrathfully around, looking to deal with the interjector.

"Come out from wherever you are, you pistle-nose. How dare you interrupt the Emperor of France. When I find you I shall have you guillotined and stick your head on a pike."

"Not in my court-room you won't – damned frog."

This from Sir Humphrey, who had awakened momentarily from a snooze. "We hang 'em in this country; none of your blood and giblets here."

"Giblets – who says giblets?" Napoleon replied, stung to attention by the inanity of the remark. "Is this a chicken you talk about? Ho – no! Your speciality is Duck, isn't it? I remember now, while I was storming Austerlitz, you were torturing some poor woman in your courtroom over some Ducks!"

Sir Humphrey staggered to his feet, and wiped a hand across his brow.

"Now don't start that again you young jacanapes. Help – where's the nurse? Help! Come and take this fiend back to his cell. He's torturing me again with his blasted ducks. How was I to know - Ducks, ducks – you can't see the capital letter when you say it. That damned Constable! Gormenghastly! It was all his fault! By gad, I should have sentenced him to twenty years while I had the opportunity."

Sir Humphrey staggered off to lie down, aiming a kick at Wellington's head as he passed the pillar where Avabite was crouching. "Out, damned Whig", he growled, and whacked him with his walking stick.

"That's right; retreat, retreat," Napoleon shouted after him, tauntingly. "The next time you sentence me to Elba, I won't go – do you hear me you old fart?"

But Sir Humphrey had retired from the field.

The most cunning inmate at Wudgi was a character that everyone called 'The Milkman'. No one knew his real name, because officially he wasn't there. He'd just wandered in there one day with a crate of milk, picked up the empties, and wandered off, looking for the exit. He couldn't get out of the front door, and the only other way was through the kitchen where there was this huge cook, with a great steaming plate of tripe and onions. Needless to say that after being bailed up four times and made to face the wall – (he never could come at tripe) – he gave up and just wandered aimlessly around the various floors and wings, looking for an exit, or for someone sane enough to show him the way out.

He began to turn up for breakfast, still in his white Milkman's coat, but looking somewhat dishevelled. He found an empty cell on the third floor, and began using that to kip between meals. After the third week he was organizing a tote on how many miles the good ship 'Wusky' would travel that day. He always won. The answer was none! The other inmates couldn't seem to get their heads around that. If it were a ship, then it must be going somewhere. Sadly, they never twigged that the 'Wusky' wasn't a ship.

After two frustrating years the milkman finally did get out, with the help of the pastry cook. He hid under the crust of a giant pie that was being prepared for the Wudgi Pig-Fest, and was wheeled past the huge cook and put into the back of a van. That was the last anyone saw of 'The Milkman'. But they do say that a few weeks later, a man looking suspiciously like 'The Milkman', in a white coat, turned up with a basket of bread on his arm, delivered his loaves and got lost in the various turrets and floors of the sanatorium trying to find his way out. This fellow became known as 'The Baker', and after three weeks began to organize a tote on how many miles the good ship 'Wusky' would travel that day. How suspicious is that, eh?

The old story that a full moon brings out the worst in lunatics was borne out in the Wusky on more than one occasion. Once a month, the place is locked down tight, and the inmates confined to their cells from 6 p.m. until 10 a.m. the following day. There's always a lot of grumbling and complaining at these times, but the rules are rigidly enforced. It gets to the stage that the inmates begin to anticipate the lock-down for some days beforehand, and on one occasion cooked up a general rebellion that began at four o'clock in the afternoon.

The first shot was to isolate the kitchen staff by locking the doors through to the main building. This cut off the kitchen and dining area from the rest of the building, along with six staff members. That left three warders wandering around the passages. These were the infamous Maude Sadismo, Johnny Slycem, and Errol Dyesome. (Gerald Baggem was on annual leave).

Slycem and Dyesome were a couple of little warts compared to Maude, who ran the place with an iron fist. The former two were usually paired together on night-shift, and to relieve the boredom would hide from each other on their rounds, wait until the other came along the darkened corridor, then jump out and yell 'Boo'. As a result of this, they had reduced each other to gibbering wrecks, and were more afraid of the inmates than they of them.

Having watched this pair through the grill from behind their locked doors, the inmates knew the game well, so when the time came that Johnny Slycem came wandering along the dim-lit corridors to lock everyone down, they were waiting for him.

"Come on Roly, time to go to your cell," said Johnny, jangling his keys. He always tried to get Roly Poly Pudding locked up first because he was a bit erratic, and had given trouble in the past. Roly was at the far end of the corridor, and now turned to face Slycem, his teeth bared. A chant started up from the gloom behind the warder, which made him immediately nervous.

"Roly Poly Pudding, got to get relief – Roly Poly Pudding, bite you with his teeth!"

Slycem spun around, meaning to silence those behind him. But there was no-one in view, just this chant wafting around corners of the corridor.

"Roly Poly Pudding, touch him at your peril – Roly Poly Pudding, already eaten Errol!"

At this, Roly began to advance on him with his hands raised like claws, and gnashing his teeth like the lunatic that he undoubtedly was. Johnny began to back off, imperceptibly at first, but then he turned and yelled over his shoulder – "Errol! Come quick! I got a problem!"

"Roly Poly Poly, sick of being pudden' – Roly Poly Poly, will eat you, though he should'n'"

As Roly approached him up the corridor, Slycem saw that Roly's face was covered in what appeared to be blood. It was actually cochineal mixed with cornflour, but did the job admirably.

"Errol! For god's sake, I'm not joking. We've got a sick one here."

Roly broke into a trot and let out a very unpudding-like snarl. That was enough for Slycem. He broke and ran, straight into the arms of Napoleon and Russell Avabite, who threw him on the floor and snatched his key ring. The last thing Johnny remembered was Roly slobbering over him before he totally passed out in blind terror. When he awoke, he was locked in a cell.

Errol Dyesome had finally heard the commotion down the other end of the corridor, and came running.

"Hang on, Johnny, I'll be there in a tick."

As he hurried past, Avabite jumped out of the shadows and yelled *"Boo!"* Errol pulled up with a jerk and turned around. Napoleon came up behind him and tapped him on the shoulder, and Errol jumped, spinning around again, in confusion. Napoleon stepped aside and Errol was faced with a demented Roly Poly, his mouth covered in blood.

"You're the pudding today, Errol! Roly Poly is very hungry!"

Errol let out a squawk, and tried to back off, but Avabite had him by the collar. Between them they had Errol in a cell and locked down before he realized what was happening. That just left Maude.

As Senior Wardress, Maude never bothered herself with lock-downs. She always let the lackeys do the dirty work. She was sitting in the office, facing into the quadrangle that made up the centre of the compound, and watching an episode of the 'Adams Family' on television. It was one of her favourite shows, and she didn't like to be disturbed. But the inmates had opened the doors to the quad, and suddenly there were people gambolling around the lawns in front of her window. Jumping to her feet, she grabbed the nightstick off the wall, and dashed out to crack a few heads.

By the time she had hurried along the corridor and out through the far door, the quad was empty. She stood for a moment, nonplussed. Had she imagined it?

Over in the shadows by the main gate, where a driveway led through from the quad to the gate, a chant started up.

"Maude Sadismo, you're a sick old witch – you're gonna get yours, you sadistic bitch!"

The chant got louder as she pursed her lips and slapped her hip with the nightstick. She was going to enjoy this.

"Maude Sadismo, you big fat pig – you couldn't get a man 'cos your arse is so big!"

At that, she let out a snarl and broke into a run. Somewhere in the shadows there were some heads to break. As she rounded the corner, she saw Roly standing in front of the gates, adopting his teeth-gnashing pose. He raised his clawlike hands as she approached, and growled, but Maude was made of sterner stuff than her staff. She swung the nightstick in the air and broke into a run.

Avabite was in the shadows, waiting, but he had no intention of tackling Maude head on. He just chose his moment and whipped out a wooden pin from its slot, a pin the size of a ten-pin bowling pin. There was a rumble up above, and Maude, in full hue and cry, was just beginning to snarl in triumph when the portcullis descended at fifty two and a half miles an hour, jack-knifing her body underneath it as her plump bottom hit the ground. It then neatly decapitated her and severed the arm holding the nightstick.

Her head rolled along the ground and came to rest at Roly's feet, staring up at him in disbelief. He bent down towards it and grinned:

"I am your worst nightmare, Maude!"

Her lips kept moving for a good thirty seconds after that, but fortunately for everyone concerned, nobody could hear the final thoughts of Maude Sadismo.

The inmates controlled the compound for three days. In that time they managed to expel the kitchen staff, barricade the back door, and seize the 27 stone cook by sheer force of numbers. They then fed her, backside first, into her own giant mincing machine, and cooked up a huge plate of tripe and onions out of her entrails.

As for Slycem and Dyesome, they resigned not long after, and left town. They weren't locals anyway, and would never have got another job in Wudgi Crossing.

Hot, Nourishing Broth

Up until now, I have studiously avoided any mention of that dread subject, sex, amongst my many chronicles of the history of Wudgi Crossing. In fact, the casual reader of these pages might imagine that the local inhabitants were so pristine and pure throughout Wudgi's history that nothing of a scandalous, libertine or prurient nature had ever occurred in that out-of-the-way place. In that, he would be mistaken.

We all know that sex is only a recent thing - that much is common knowledge! It did not manifest itself in Victorian times, because Queen Victoria would not have stood for it! After Albert died she went into mourning for thirty years, wore black, and abstained from anything that might bring the British Empire into disrepute - and she expected her subjects to follow suit.

All the confinements in those days were immaculate conceptions – I know this, because my great-grandmother confided as much to me when she was on her deathbed. Men were regarded as filthy brutes who spent their lives attempting to glimpse a sight of a nicely turned ankle, or in extreme cases, a well-shaped calf. They were foiled in this by the full-length dresses and petticoats of the day, which rarely rose above the toe of the boot.

Legs became such a fetish at that time that the legs of tables and chairs, especially the nicely turned legs of Queen Anne furniture, had to be covered by material draperies in case they incited men to lust. (Though what a man was going to accomplish lusting after a wardrobe, I really don't know).

Women were kept on pedestals in those days, a system which might have suited over-crowded London, but which was very inconvenient in a place like Wudgi. As the ceilings of the cottages were so low, it must have been nigh on impossible to stand crouched on a pedestal all day, head pressed against the tin – (no doubt, that's how that particular ceiling material came to be known as 'pressed tin'.) As a result, most of the pedestals in Wudgi stood out in the backyard. It must have been a comic sight seeing all these dutiful wives, standing in rows, from backyard to backyard, chatting happily with each other, and freezing into a silent decorum whenever a man came into view.

Later, of course, these pedestals were hidden from the vulgar view by little square boxes with doors on them, and to make them as functional as they were necessary, it became common practice to incorporate with these pedestals a 'long drop', so a dual purpose could be achieved. This entailed the digging of a hole about thirty feet deep, and changing the shape of the pedestal to comply with its other purpose. Later on the common term for these additions became 'toilet' – by which time women had given up the practice of standing on them for hours at a time, as they were now too hard to balance on.

After the Pankhurst sisters did their bit for the emancipation of women, things began to relax somewhat, and women were allowed to come inside during the day when their husbands weren't there, to do things like wash dishes, clean house, make the beds and cook an evening meal. No doubt this was a great step forward, as it released women from petty tyrannies like the pedestal, which they were now allowed to sit on, giving them equal rights with their husbands.

But all this is Victorian and Edwardian history, and by the early teens of the twentieth century, women had essentially cast off their shackles and were acting independently of their menfolk.

Arabella Silkenshanks was the first woman to

attempt a little independent business enterprise, with her shopfront premises in the main street. She didn't have a lot of money, so decided to paint her own shop window to save the cost of the signwriter. It would have been better if she'd paid. Signwriters tended to be men of the world, and she would have no doubt, been given better advice if she'd consulted one first.

As it was, on the morning she opened for business, the good citizens hurried past her premises, shocked looks on their faces, and by ten o'clock of that morning a constable had arrived to take Miss Silkenshanks into custody. As it was a quiet day in the local court, she soon found herself before a magistrate, blushing, and attempting to justify herself.

The numerous charges included: 'Setting up a house of ill-repute, indulging in infamous practices, inciting men into immoral acts, acting contrary to the ordinances of the Wudgi Crossing Town Council, and permitting an immoral sign to be displayed on a public building.'

"What have you to say to these charges," said the Right Honourable Ralph Come-Uply, looking down grimly at her from the Judges bench. He was of the old Victorian mould, and it was obvious before the hearing began that Miss Silkenshanks would get little sympathy from any court he presided over.

"I don't understand what all the fuss is about. No doubt, a lot of this has come about because I'm a woman. If a man had come up with the idea, I suppose it would have been all right," she said, primly.

"No, madame, it most certainly would *not* have been all right. But there again, no man would have lowered himself to such a level."

"It's true that this is not usually the type of establishment a man would think to involve himself in, this being woman's work...."

At this there was a gasp from the body of the court, and the Right Honourable blanched in response.

"...but I still fail to understand what is deemed immoral. Surely, those gentlemen without wives of their own would appreciate being able to come along to my humble establishment and be catered for at the hands of a gentlewoman. For just a few pence..."

"Silence, Madame. I fear that you are about to damn yourself out of your own mouth."

Come-Uply glared at Constable Pilchard, and

told him to take the stand.

"Please give your evidence, constable – and spare us nothing!"

"Aherr-umm," said Pilchard, clearing his throat. "At about 9.15a.m. I was approached by Mrs. Evelyn Repugnance, who appeared to be in great distress! She was making 'whooping' noises like she was having hysterics, or trying to get her breath."

"Whooping noises, Constable. Please illustrate what you mean."

"Well, she was going 'whoop-whoop', then saying something which I couldn't catch, then 'whoop-whoop' again. It was some minutes before I could calm her down enough to get the gist of what she was saying."

"Which was, Constable?"

"That there was a new business in town that I should be looking into. She said it was infamous, and that the ladies around here would have to keep their menfolk under lock and key if it was allowed to continue. I asked her what sort of business she was talking about, and she just went bright red, your honour, and said something about -" here he consulted his notebook – "those words will never pass my lips, Constable."

"So did she eventually 'let those words pass her lips', Constable?"

"No, your honour. But then Mrs. Annabelle Grimace came leaping through the door in a terrible state, jumping up and down on one foot, and looking totally disgusted.

"And she said…"

"That it was a disgrace what some women would stoop to, and that if this was what emancipation meant, then she was 'agin it.'"

"Did she elaborate, Constable?"

"No, your Honour. Well not in so many words. She did say that it would bring disgrace upon the town of Wudgi Crossing, and that if we wanted our main street choked up with tour buses full of men's clubs, then we deserved all we got."

"And then what happened, constable – I must say, this is all getting extremely vague."

"Yes, sir. That's what I thought at the time. Then a delegation of women piled in through the door, consisting of the President of the Temperance League, Mrs. Abomination, the secretary of the Knitting Circle, Mrs Loathsome, the Treasurer of the Votes For Women Committee, Mrs. Detestation, and Mrs. Abhorrent, Mrs. Insufferable, and Mrs. Disagreeable. They all seemed to be of the one view..."

"And what was that, constable?"

"That Miss Silkenshanks should be arrested immediately, and placed before this court.

There was a murmur of assent from the body of the court, and a few 'hear-hear's'."

"That will be enough," said Come-Uply, banging with his gavel. "I will not tolerate impudence from the gallery. Continue, Constable Pilchard."

"Well, in the end, your honour, I decided to go and look for myself, and when I did, I was shocked."

"Yes... go on, go on! You are keeping this court in suspense, constable."

"I approached the shopfront from the street, as any customer would do, and after reading the sign, went straight in."

"And what happened then?"

"Miss Silkenshanks approached me, and said: 'Ah, my first customer. What can I entice you with this fine morning, Constable?'"

"Is that right. Please continue, Constable Pilchard."

"She said there were some fifteen variations on the 'menu', and I could have my pick. I must admit, I was shocked!"

"I can understand why – 'Menu' indeed!"

"I said, do you realise that you are indulging in an illegal activity, and that you are the subject of a number of complaints from women in the town?"

"What did she say to that, constable?"

"She said that the old biddies in Wudgi were just jealous of her entrepreneurial skills, and that they would have done it themselves if they'd thought of it first."

"So she impugned the good character of the Wudgi ladies, I see. This is becoming more serious than I thought."

"This is ridiculous," Arabella interjected. "So far you haven't given one good reason why I should be so rudely arrested, and dragged into this court."

"Prisoner at the bar, be silent, or I shall be forced to gaol you for contempt. You have been charged with -" here the magistrate consulted his notes, and then his notes of the evidence so far. He frowned for a moment, then turned to Pilchard and commented:

"She's right, you know. There's not one hard statement concerning what this prisoner is alleged to have done in breaking the law. What *is* this about, Pilchard?"

"I should have thought it obvious, your honour. The sign on the shop said it all."

"Oh – the sign! Well, what about the sign. I've seen no mention of what the sign actually said in your evidence so far."

"Well, I hardly like to repeat it in – er – mixed company, your honour," remarked the constable, shuffling his feet, and indicating the ladies in the gallery.

"I'm sure it can't be that horrific," replied Come-Uply, showing his annoyance for the first time. "Please tell the court what the sign on the prisoner's window said."

"It said – um – 'Mam'selle Silkenshanks Homely Brothel', your honour."

The Right Honourable Come-Uply went red in the face, then sat back, looking grim.

"So! The evidence is clear enough. What do you have to say to that, madame?"

"What's wrong with that? What else would you call a shop selling hot, nourishing broth?"

Arabella looked defiantly around the court-room, as a series of titters began.

"Hot, nourishing broth? You mean broth – as in soup," said Come-Uply, slowly, a smile gathering at the corners of his mouth.

"Yes; broth - soup. You call a coffee shop a café, a grocer has a Grocery! Tanners work in a Tannery. I decided to call my broth shop a brothel. What's wrong with that?"

At this, the entire court erupted in a wave of laughter, and even Come-Uply was seen to grin for the first time ever, as he banged his gavel and yelled for silence in the court.

"I take it you have lived a sheltered life, Miss Silkenshanks," the magistrate commented, in a more kindly manner than before.

Flustered at the laughter, Arabella began to blush. "Yes – I – lived at the convent until I was thirteen, then I went to stay with an elderly aunt. What's that got to do with anything?"

"Your education was interrupted, I take it. Your knowledge of the English language is rather limited."

"I get by," she replied, flushing at this attack on her intellect.

"Madame, a brothel is a house of ill-fame. It is a place frequented by prostitutes."

There was a deadly silence as Arabella Silkenshanks took this in. Her jaw dropped, and she turned the colour of a ripe beetroot. Then she put her hands up to her face, and burst into tears.

"I think we have heard enough. Case dismissed," Come-Uply said, before rushing out to his private rooms where he remained chuckling to himself for the next half an hour.

Arabella raced home and packed a bag. She left on the West Coast Bus at 1.00 p.m. that day, after painting over that terrible sign on her window.

No-one in Wudgi ever heard of her again, though old Mrs. Pilchard, the constable's wife, did say that many years later she spotted someone who looked like her in Port Augusta one day. This woman had a different name, and was seen to be working in a rare bird shop, called 'Mrs. Braziers Tits'.

Hong Kong Flu

Just out of Wudgi on the Adelaide Road, there is a strange looking building with all sorts of carvings and inscriptions all over it in some foreign lingo. It has arches and a courtyard, all overgrown now with ivy and mile-a-minute, but it must have been something to look at in its prime. It once belonged to the Cuckoo family, who have long since travelled on from their humble Wudgi beginnings.

Ah-So Koo was the first member of this family to stumble into Wudgi Crossing, in the mistaken belief that it was a gold-mining town. When he discovered that there was no gold, and no jobs for 'Chinee Go' Digger', he opened a Chinese Laundry in the main street. A few pleasant years went by, with Ah-So Koo building a flourishing business, and in his spare time, fishing in the Wudgi Creek – in season of course.

The fact that there were no fish in the Wudgi Creek did not deter Ah-So Koo one bit. Each Sunday winter's morning you could find him on the Creek banks near the bridge, casting his line out and reeling it in at regular intervals; empty of course. When questioned about why he did it, he would reply: 'Good for contemplaysung.' Thinking that this was some Chinese bit of wisdom from Confucius, the locals left him alone.

What they didn't realize was that another Chinese family had taken up residence on the other side of the creek, and from where he sat the wily Ah-So could keep tabs on their beautiful daughter Sung Long Koo, who would play on the opposite creek bank. (The fact that their surnames were the same fascinated Ah-So, and he saw it as a sign from the gods that he had been sent a flower to brighten his life).

As the years went on, Sung Long Koo got to marriageable age, and Ah-So was heard to sigh long and hard in her direction, whenever she brought her Chinese laundry into his Chinese Laundry. That was the most that he was allowed to do to announce his interest, as in China they have their own way of doing things, and this takes time.

After the third sighing, and the third fluttering of the eyelashes, Sung Long Koo was able to go home and tell her parents that she had met a man who had intentions of wooing her. Could she obtain their permission to be wooed. Her father immediately objected. It was the done thing for fathers to object, the culturally accepted response.

'Who this flunky?' said her father, angrily. 'Not some Euloplean pluckhead who tlink lat Chinee girl be lipe for plucking!' he added, indignantly. 'I shlow him,' said Hung Long Koo, who immediately packed a bag to set out on a journey to the Chinese Laundry in main street.

Long did Sung Long and her mother, Hong Kong Flu wail and make loud beseechings, all quite culturally correct, to try and stop Hung Long setting out on his journey. Ah-So could hear them quite clearly on the other side of the creek, giving him the option of getting out there and then, or steeling himself to face the father-in-law to be. He decided to stay, and face the music.

For two days Hung Long travelled, stopping every twenty-two paces as required in the 'Confucius Say...', a little yellow handbook that all Confucianists referred to for every major decision in their lives. He would stop, light a joss stick, mutter a short prayer of manhood and check to see if Hong Kong's Chinese sandwiches looked any more appetising than the last time he looked. At noon on the second day, Hung Long Koo threw open the door of the Chinese Laundry and called out - 'I am Hung Long...'

Ah-So stood quaking behind the counter. He

looked and looked, and kept his back tightly against the wall just in case he was. Finally he said – 'Ah-So...' And waited for the response.

Hung Long turned red in the face. Then he muttered, his voice rising in anger: 'Ar-sole! Ar-sole! You dare call your future fartler-in-law Ar-Sole? I teach you lesson, you daughter plucker dog, you!' He then threw his hamper down on the counter and ruffled through it, looking for his 'Confucius Say...' to instruct him in the best way to proceed.

'No no no, not Ar-Sole!' stammered Ah-So, realizing his predicament. 'I am Ah-So Koo, and would beg for your dlaughter's hand in malliage.'

'Ah! So...' Hung Long replied. "I see! You so Cool! All you young ones think you so cool! But not enough! What your name, So Cool?'

'My name,' Ah-So muttered, slowly and desperately now, the beads of sweat breaking out on his forehead, 'is Ah....So....Koo! Ah...So...Koo!'

A light seemed to glimmer behind the little yellow eyes of Hung Long Koo.

'So... you Koo too! Ah-So Koo! Is that what you say?'

Ah-So nodded in relief. 'Ah-So Koo. Pleased to

meet fartler of Sung Long at last.' He put his hands together in the age-old Chinese greeting, and bowed his head in respect.

Hung Long made some sound like 'Hurrumpppphhh!' and stood there on his dignity, not knowing for the moment how to respond. Then he offered Ah-So one of Hong Kong Flu's sandwiches.

Ah-So took a tentative bite, then realised why it had taken Hung Long two days to travel across the creek and up the main street. 'Blaked Bleans,' he said through a mouthful of mush, trying to smile as he looked for a suitable bin to spit it into. Hung Long must have had the runs for two days.

'So...Ah-So! You wish mally my dlaughter, Sung Long. How I know you good for her, look after her plopelly? This your Laundly?'

'Yes, velly good laundly! Only one in Wudgi Clossing. Velly lich!'

'Velly lich! Ah! That all light then. But name not good. Koo! Same name but difflent.'

At this point I should enlighten the reader that Ah-So's 'Koo' was pronounced slightly differently to Hung Low's 'Koo'. Noticeable only to the oriental ear, the former was more of a 'Cu', where the latter was a definite 'Koo'. By the time a marriage agreement had been arranged between the two, it was agreed that the surnames would have to be hyphenated. So Ah-So Koo and his bride, Sung Long Koo became in course of time Mr and Mrs Koo-Koo. Two generations later, now fully integrated Australians, the name became Cuckoo, and that's the way it has remained.

The marriage agreement was a fairly complicated affair, as Chinese agreements usually are, and there was a clause in which Ah-So was required to help Hong Kong Flu, Hung Long's wife, start up a Chinese Restaurant in the town.

Due to various misunderstandings, however, language differences and personality problems, the *'Hong Kong Flu Chinese Restaurant'* never did get off the ground in Wudgi Crossing. It certainly opened for business, and the décor was 'velly Chinee', with gold dragons and red tablecloths and funny Chinese characters over the doorway, but Wudgi folk, for one reason or another, failed to frequent the place, and after three weeks it closed down.

Argument has it that the simple Wudgi folk were not game enough to risk a dose of Hong Kong Flu, and so stayed and cooked at home. But what certainly didn't help was Hung Long Koo standing at the front door, inviting people in with the immortal words – 'Please tly good Chinee Gobstopper. I am Hung Long!'

'I'm pretty well hung meself,' said one passer-by, backing away at speed, 'but I don't stand on street corners and shout about it!'

Toad in the Hall

On a tiny smallholding, several miles from Wudgi Crossing, there once lived a family called Godbothering, who had occupied the said smallholding since before Mick McGurk's infamous cattle drive in 1862. They had actually been in occupation since 1848, when Grandfather Leopold Annaheim Wankelwurzel had raced his bullocks to the top of a nearby hill, looked out over the valley below and said: 'Zis vill do! I claim zis valley in ze name of ze Imperial German Emperor, und dedicate it to Luther. Ve vill build ze church!'

By the time other settlers caught up with the Wankelwurzels', both the Lutheran Church and the valley were well established, and the Wankelwurzel family of thirty-six daughters and one son were firmly in control. The one son was Herman, and he had married an Elsa Pumpernickel that he'd had shipped out from Cologne as a domestic servant.

As the Wankelwurzel family were strict Lutherans, and tended to dress in black and white in all seasons and walk around with German Bibles under their arms, the other settlers in the area began to snipe at them; one of the favourite terms of abuse being – 'They're just a pack of Godbotherer's.' When this came to the ears of Herman, who was about to become a father for the first time, he flung his head back in a pose of godly righteousness and said: 'Is zat so? In zat case ve vill wear zis name wiz honour. From now on, ze middle name of all Wankelwurzels' vill be 'Godbothering!'

So it was that when Herman's son was born, the idea was to christen him Adam Leopold Godbothering Wankelwurzel in the nearby Lutheran Church. Adam was the first Wankelwurzel born on Australian soil, so the whole community was looking forward to the christening.

The church was presided over by Pastor Gunter, an aging man of the cloth who had seen better days. He was frankly, an old dodderer who often fell asleep in the middle of his own sermons, and had to be awoken by the organist, who would let out a blast in 'F' sharp from the pressure in the bellows. There were often more 'F' sharps than hymns in those days, but when the 'F' sharps began to intrude into the hymns themselves, the church elders finally began to look at ways of retiring Gunter without hurting his feelings.

As an initial step, they recruited a junior Pastor to come in on an *ad hoc* basis, when Gunter wasn't feeling well. He had the title of the 'Under' Pastor, while Gunter gloried in that of the 'Over' Pastor.

On the day of the christening, Pastor Gunter was standing on the steps of the Church, ostensibly to greet the churchgoers as they entered, but in actual fact, fast asleep on his feet. This was not a good portent. The organist whistled an 'F' sharp as he walked by, and Gunter staggered in behind him to lead the service. The 'Under' Pastor was unavailable that day, so there was no one to fill in should Pastor Gunter need a relief.

Everything was going swimmingly until the infant, held by Herman over the font, was being baptised. Gunter got to the part 'I christen thee....', then had to stop and consult the child's father.

"Adam Leopold Godbothering......" growled Herman in a whisper. Surely the old devil hadn't forgotten already. Gunter started again:

"I christen thee Adam........ Leopold... Godbothering...."

Herman waited for a few moments, then hissed 'Wankelwurzel.... Wankelwurzel!'

Pastor Gunter just stood there like a statue, to all intents and purposes sound asleep.

"I said Wankelwurzel, Pastor!" Herman prodded Gunter in the chest with his finger.

Down went the Pastor like the wreck of the Hesperus. Spreadeagled at the base of the font, it was soon established that the 'Over' Pastor had just passed over.

What a dilemma! There was no-one else suitably cloth'd to take over his duties, so the christening party broke up in disarray. The name that was entered in the book was Adam Leopold Godbothering, and despite pleas, threats and an attempt at bribery, that's exactly how it stayed.

The next Pastor, the newly promoted 'Under' Pastor, was approached with a view to correcting the mistake, but the attitude was taken that this would not reflect kindly on Pastor Gunter's memory, and so the elders directed that nothing was to be changed. The proud name of Wankelwurzel was thus consigned to history.

Adam Godbothering grew up to have five sons, and each of these in turn had five sons, all 'Godbotherer's', and all Godbotherings. Three generations later, the remnants of the family had dispersed across Australia, the only one's remaining in the valley being a Gordon Godbothering and his wife Lucy.

This couple were certainly not 'Godbotherer's', not even Lutherans! It could be questioned, indeed, whether they were even christians, as they were completely self-centred, avaricious, grasping, greedy and slothful – all those nice things! For some reason, Lucy thought that she was a cut above everyone else, and so refused to soil her hands with anything like housework. Gordon, for reasons of *his* own, thought he was above working for a living, and spent his time gainfully, borrowing from the neighbours what he had not been able to steal. Needless to say, it was not many years before the two found their presence in the valley an embarrassment to others, who would regularly slam and bolt their doors whenever the Godbotherings' appeared in the driveway.

Meanwhile, In the nearby settlement of Wudgi Crossing, the Anglican Church had just appointed a new minister; the Reverend Godby Luvus Godbothering, a seventh son of a Victorian branch of the family, whose calling was dictated both by his name, and by his lowly position in the hierarchy.

"Edgar will inherit the land," his father had proclaimed. "That's only fitting, as he is the eldest. Brian will make a career in the military. Leo's a bit funny, so he can stay home and help his mother with the embroidery. John gets the cottage at the end of the south paddock. Eric has married into money, so we can forget about him. Marcus is doing okay with his gardening round, so he can have the lawnmower and the whipper snipper. He can even have the old trailer behind the shed. But Godby? What are we going to do with Godby?"

He thought for a minute, then straightened up and raised one finger in the light of inspiration.

"I know! He can go into the church. We could do with a vicar in the family, save on all those fees for weddings, christenings and burials. Yes, that could be quite handy."

What Godby thought about this has not been recorded, though he was only eight at the time. He did know that whenever his father shortened his name to 'God', and yelled it at the top of his voice, it sent a little shiver down his spine; and that when he added 'God Luvus', he used to break out in a sweat. This usually meant his father was angry about something. Godby was probably glad to get away to the Anglican Seminary in the end, if just for a little peace.

The end result of seven years of study was a shy, retiring little man, who was timid to the n'th.

degree. After some years of service in various parishes, he was just the sort of vicar that Wudgi Crossing could get along with, as most of the population were out and out barbarians anyway. So quietly, the Reverend Godby Luvus Godbothering settled, barely noticeably, into the manse.

He had not been installed more than a fortnight when, by chance, Lucy Godbothering sailed into Wudgi for a spot of shopping. In passing she could not help but notice that the new incumbent's surname was the same as her husband's, and when she returned to the valley, she mentioned the fact to Gordon.

"Must be a cousin," said Gordon. "Must be! The Godbotherings all started in this valley, and even if he does come from interstate, he's still one of us. Maybe we should pay him a visit."

"Perhaps we should even stay awhile," said Lucy, "get to know him. He may know the whereabouts of other cousins of yours in Victoria."

So it was that the following week, the Reverend Godby received a letter in the post, alerting him to the imminent arrival of his cousins, who would be calling in to congratulate him on his appointment to the parish. As they would be arriving somewhat late in the afternoon, could he possibly put them up until the following day to save them the inconvenience of having to book in at the Wudgi Arms?

The alarm bells should have rung loud and clear at this point, but the Rev. Godby, being an unsuspicious soul, and being a man of charity, returned a note saying that would be fine, and that he was looking forward to meeting other members of the family. He added a subscript that he had always understood the family had originated in this region, but was not really up on the history of it all. This was all the opening the Godbotherings needed.

The following day, Gordon and Lucy turned up in a battered old car that looked as if they'd purchased it from the wreckers. They sat it in the driveway of the manse, blocking off the gate, and all access for other church workers, who had to scale the fence to get in.

After the initial introductions, and a brief tour of the house, Lucy settled herself in Godby's comfortable armchair in the lounge, while Gordon spread himself across the couch, leaving Godby to perch himself on a chair brought in from the kitchen.

"You're nicely set up here, Godby. Very nicely set up. Got a housekeeper have you? You'd need a housekeeper in a house this size. A cook too! Have you got a cook, Godby?"

Godby assured her that he didn't have a cook, that his own needs in that area were meagre in the extreme. He got by with a microwave and a toaster. Lucy looked shocked.

"A man in your position, Vicar, should be better looked after. They have a terrible job filling these out of the way parishes you know. If I were you, I would demand it."

Godby laughed deprecatingly, and shook his head. "Oh no, I could never do that... er... Lucy. My parishioners would think I was decadent."

Lucy gave out a jolly laugh.

"And what's wrong with a bit of decadence, that's what I say, Vicar." Godby looked somewhat uncomfortable at that suggestion.

Gordon lit up a cigarette, and flicked the match into the fireplace. Godby waved his hand at him to try and catch his attention.

"We don't smoke in the manse, Gordon."

Gordon took a deep drag on his cigarette, and blew out a ring of smoke.

"Don't you? Well, good on you, Godby, it's good to see that someone in the family's kicked the habit. Me? I'm a lost cause. I reckon it'll give me up before I manage to get around to it." He laughed, and blew another smoke ring.

"No, you don't understand... No-one smokes in the manse, Gordon." Godby was a little agitated.

"Don't they? Well, who would have believed there were so many reformed smokers in Wudgi, eh, Lucy? I hope it's not catching!"

"No hope of that with you," Lucy sniffed. 'He's a typical Godbothering, Godby. Talk 'til your blue in the face, and that's all you'll get. Which reminds me; a cup of coffee would go down well, wouldn't it, Gordon?"

"I'd kill for a cup of coffee, Lucy. Haven't had one since we set off. Still, you don't want me to make it, do you?'

"Oh, don't be silly, Gordon. We couldn't make free with the Reverend's kitchen just like that."

Gordon threw his cigarette into the fireplace. Godby gave a slight sigh of relief, and turned to Lucy.

"Oh, where's my manners. I forgot you'd had a bit of a journey – I should have offered. How do you take your coffee? White?"

"With two sugars," said Lucy, "and three for his lordship over there. And don't be stingy with the milk.'

Godby gave her a nervous smile, then went to the kitchen to put on the kettle. The moment he left the room, Gordon got up and wandered around the room. He checked the books in the bookcase, picked up and inspected the brass ornaments on the mantlepiece, and was over by the writing bureau when Godby returned with the coffee. Godby cleared his throat, and put the coffee down.

"Here's your coffee, Gordon," Lucy said, sounding a warning note. Gordon turned.

"Just admiring your bureau, Godby. Chinese isn't it? Nice carving."

"Thai,' said Godby, "and if you don't mind, Gordon, a bureau is a private thing…"

"Oh, yeah," said Gordon, going back to the couch. "That's what I was thinking, too. I suppose you get all sorts of nosey parkers coming in here, looking through your bureau. I'd keep the lid shut if I were you, Godby. You never know with these people."

"Errr… exactly," said Godby, walking over to shut the bureau. He even made a show of locking the top and removing the key.

"Good move my man," said Gordon, nodding wisely. "Keep that locked. You never know, do you Luce?"

Lucy tucked her feet under her in the armchair, without removing her shoes. "No, you have to be careful around here, Godby. After all, these people in Wudgi Crossing – you don't know them yet, do you."

"Oh, they seem to be pretty nice people," Godby mumbled, feeling that a tad of loyalty was called for.

"Pretty nice on the surface..." Lucy said, with a note of hesitation in her voice. "But if you knew some of the things that have gone on here over the years..." She pursed her lips, and shook her head, pointedly, at Gordon.

"Oooh yes, if you only knew...." Gordon reciprocated, then tut-tutted through his teeth.

Godby was at a loss for a reply. He made to get up.

"Oh, yes, thanks for reminding us! You're off to get our bags, are you. Make sure you get my blue overnight one out of the boot, Godby, there's a dear. Well, give him the keys, Gordon, he can't do anything without the keys."

"The bags... you want me to..."

"You're a champion, Godby. Of course, my arthritis plays me up something awful these days, otherwise I'd come out and help."

"Now you'll do no such thing, will he, Godby? No! See!... Godby agrees with me. It's no good damaging yourself at your age, Gordon."

"And what age would that be, Gordon," said Godby, somewhat puzzled.

"Forty two now, Godby. Old age creeping up on me! Not like you, young fella."

"I'm thirty eight," said Godby, staring at Gordon.

"Just my point! God, the thirties, what I'd give..."

"Don't hold him up, Gordon, it's getting dark, and I'd like to get settled. After all, he's got to get dinner yet, haven't you, Godby? Which reminds me, I'm ravenous, Gordon."

"Well, if you'd like to use the kitchen to cook yourselves something...."

"Oh, listen to him, Gordon. No, what?... Me cook? Dear me, you are behind the times, Godby. I couldn't do that. Never have in fact, have I Gordon," she said proudly. "No, I can honestly say that cooking is something I never really came to terms with, Godby. Deary me, imagine what it would do to my nails." She held up a manicured hand and inspected it at leisure. "No, but that's all right, Godby, we'll just have what you're having. We don't mind slumming it on the odd occasion, do we, Gordon?"

"Nah! I'm easy," said Gordon. "Whatever you stick on the table, cuz, we won't complain. We're not demanding sorts of people. Easy to get on with, eh Luce?"

"Just let him get the bags, Gordon."

The following night, Godby came back from a parishioners meeting to find them waiting for him. The car was still jammed in the driveway, and the lounge was starting to become cluttered with items from the Godbothering's suitcases. Lucy's ample brassiere's were hanging on the fireguard, drying, while Gordon had kicked his shoes under the table, dumped his jacket on the couch, thrown his tie on the floor, and left the daily paper strewn all over the table. But it was what was standing next to the paper that caused Godby's eyes to almost pop out.

The Reverend Godby had one little weakness that I haven't mentioned to this point. Godby was fond of a glass of wine at the end of the day, and he prided himself on some of the wines he had managed to collect over the years, thinking them a considerable investment. Standing next to the paper, and looking very empty, was a bottle of his prized 1968 Shiraz.

"What.... what-what-what-what...." he stuttered at Gordon, pointing a shaking finger at his prized bottle. Gordon looked down at his half empty glass, and threw the rest down his throat before replying.

"Good drop, that! I saw it in the rack there, and it was obviously getting on a bit. Another few months and it would probably have been off, Godby. You're lucky I drank it first."

"But... but-but-but.... That Shiraz was never meant for drinking...."

"What – you thought it had gone off already! Well, I'm not surprised. I mean, 1968. That's what I call optimistic, Godby."

"No... that's what I call four hundred dollars," said Godby, wearily. "I bought it for eighty dollars twelve years ago. It was now worth four hundred!"

"Well bugger me! It just goes to show, don't it? If I'd known that, I'd have drunk it a lot more slowly, I'll tell you that," said Gordon, chuckling.

"I hope that's the only bottle you've opened today..." said Godby, looking around. Lucy shifted uncomfortably in Godby's chair, and pulled a face.

"Well Godby, we didn't think you'd mind. That Port was pretty old, too."

"Not the '48 Port," Godby groaned. "Not the '48 Port!"

Lucy grimaced, in an attempt to lighten the situation. "It was terrible anyway. It took us a whole hour to drink it, it was that strong."

Godby stood for a moment as if paralysed, then turned and stomped out of the room without another word.

Later, at McSoufflé's Restaurant, the vicar allowed himself to unburden himself to the restaurateur. "I should have let you have it, Angus, when you offered me three fifty."

Angus McSoufflé looked glumly at the vicar, and shook his head.

"And a '48 Port, you said." Angus shook his head again, and sighed.

"Yes, a '48 Port. But that's not the worst of it, Angus. I mean, I don't know how long they intend to stay. I can't just throw them out, they're cousins, after all."

"Cousins from hell by the sound of it," said McSoufflé, unimpressed.

"You should see the place. They're turning it

into a rubbish dump, and neither of them will lift a finger to do anything. I've never known anyone like it. They expect me to wait on them hand and foot. She doesn't cook, he doesn't work; neither of them do any housework. They tell me that their car won't start, and they haven't the money to get a mechanic to it for a fortnight.'

At this, the vicar seized Angus by the collar with both hands. He was beside himself.

"A fortnight, Angus! A fortnight! I can't stand it, I'll go crazy! May God forgive me, but I just have to get rid of them. I've never felt so helpless before."

Angus pried the vicar's hands off his collar and sat him down.

"You need a drink, Godby. Here, I'll get you a scotch, and then we'll work out a plan of action. But don't worry, we'll sort it out."

True to his word, Angus sent the vicar home and put the first part of his plan into action. He paid a visit to Sarah Wartnose, the local witch.

"I understand you'll been doing a bit of smuggling, Sarah," he said, as he ducked under the door jamb to get into her kitchen. Sarah stuck her pointy nose in the air, and looked at him

201

suspiciously.

"What are we talking about here," she enquired.

"Toads! Queensland toads, cane toads Sarah! Better known as Argentine toads, the big fellows."

Sarah pulled a face.

"So you know! Oh well, the local ones are poor specimens. If you want to get a half-decent spell going, you need a good-sized toad."

"You do know that it's illegal to import cane toads into South Australia. You could go to jail."

"Fat chance of that," she snapped. "By the time I've finished with them, they don't look like toads anymore."

"That's exactly what I wanted to talk to you about. I understand you have a magic spell to get rid of unwanted guests, and it requires a large toad as the main ingredient."

Sarah suddenly cackled, and Angus took a step back. He never felt totally comfortable with Sarah, or with her enemy O'Malley, over the garden fence.

"It's not so much a spell as a recipe," she cackled. "You run a restaurant; you could do this! If I give you the method, you can handle it for yourself, without involving me."

"I'll need a toad," said McSoufflé, as if striking a deal.

"And you'll promise to stay out of my affairs?"

"I promise!"

She went out the back and came in with a toad fifteen inches high, and Ugly!

Two days later, after priming the vicar and arranging a little dinner party for four, McSoufflé turned up at the back door of the manse with a large cardboard box. He let himself into the kitchen, while Godby ushered the cousins into a small front room, sparsely furnished except for a table and four chairs. There were candles on the table, and a nice lace cloth. Settling them in their chairs, Godby poured them both a drink, and then excused himself to go to the kitchen.

"Now just you relax, have a couple of drinks, unwind a bit. I've got the chef on the job, and he might be a little while."

Lucy preened herself and picked up her glass.

"Well this is a nice surprise, Godby. You certainly know how to treat your guests…. Doesn't he, Gordon," she said, giving Gordon a nudge with her elbow.

"Uhhh! Oh, yeah! Very nice of you, Godby,"

was Gordon's response. He had been in a bad mood since the vicar had locked away the remainder of his wine, and hidden all the matches in the house. Since then he had moped about, looking for things to pinch before they left. Lucy pulled a face as Godby left the room, emptied her glass and pulled a wry face.

"Oh well, it's not a '68 Shiraz, but it'll do. You might as well get stuck in, Gordon." She held her glass out to him, and he filled it for her, then took a swig out of the bottle.

"I wonder what this 'mystery dish' is, I hope it's a steak," he said. "I'm sick of living on baked beans on toast."

"As long as it doesn't cost us anything, Gordon," said Lucy.

In the kitchen, the plan was well under way.

"Are you sure this is going to do the trick," said Godby.

"You'll never see them again," Angus replied, with a grin. "Just make sure you're not in the room when I deliver the main course."

Godby returned with the entrees, and sat down with them, making an excuse for Angus, saying he was tied up for the moment. They each tackled a prawn cocktail, and made small talk, while Godby noted that the first bottle was already empty, and Lucy was being obvious, playing with her glass.

"I'll crack us another bottle once I've finished this entrée," said Godby. "I don't know about you, but I can't wait for this mystery dish."

"What – don't you even know what it is?" said Lucy.

"No – no, I'm as much in the dark as you," said Godby. This was basically true, as he had told Angus just to do it, not to tell him about it. The Reverend Godby Godbothering was somewhat at odds with the Wine Collector Godby, in that the Reverend had a God to answer to, whereas Godby the Wino had only his anger and desperation. "No doubt, we'll soon find out."

He excused himself and met Angus in the passageway, hurrying toward the dining room. He was carrying the dish under a domed cover, so Godby never even got to see it. He watched Angus disappear into the room, then come rushing out carrying the lid with him and slamming the door behind him. There was a loud sizzling from within the room, and then a muffled explosion, which literally blew the door out into the passage.

Godby stood with his mouth open as his two

cousins staggered into the passageway, absolutely dripping with some very smelly matter, which had coated them from head to foot.

Godby took a step towards them and Gordon yelled: "Stay away from us, you maniac. Don't you come near us."

"Look at my hair," howled Lucy, as they both staggered out through the front door, and tottered up the driveway.

Twenty seconds later there was the sound of a starter motor turning over, the car sprang into life, and the tyres squealed as Gordon took off in the direction of the valley. Godby never saw either of them again.

Two weeks later, after extensive cleaning operations, Godby approached Angus out of curiosity and asked him to reveal the mystery.

"Do you really want to know?" said Angus, with a smirk.

"Yes! I think I do. I can't stop thinking about it."

"In that case, I'll give you the recipe," said Angus, and pulled out a piece of paper from a folder behind the counter. Here is the recipe he gave the Reverend that day.

Toad In The Hall

Ingredients:

    1 large Queensland Bug-Eyed Toad
    1 Horny Skinned Grampus (Small)
    ½ Pint Lavatory Cleaner (Powder Form)
    2 Packets Baking Soda
    ½ Combustible Trifle (Brandy Based)
    1 Glass Tube
    1 Long Handled Squeegee
    1 Long Handled Wooden Spoon (earthed)

Method:

Carefully feed the Toad the two packs of Baking Soda, using the glass tube to blow it well down into the back of the throat. Take the trifle, which should be well dried out, and baste slowly over a cup of soup (any flavour). Then sift the result and blend carefully together with the lavatory cleaner until black smoke appears – DON'T LET IT EXPLODE! Skin the grampus and pack the blended paste into the skin, using a wooden spoon earthed to the nearest convenient socket. (Should you use an unearthed spoon the resulting electrostatic charge could well demolish your kitchen).

Taking the packed Grampus skin, ram this thoughtfully down the Toad's throat, using the spoon handle as a rammer if required. Swiftly then, take the startled Toad by the scruff of the neck and thrust it into the microwave for 30 seconds.

You must now proceed at speed, or the element of surprise will be lost. Seize the Toad by the lips, being sure to hold them tightly together to avoid any involuntary rejection of the Grampus skin, and race through the house until you reach the doorway of the room in which your unwelcome visitors sit.

With the cry 'Toad in the Hall', fling the beast into the middle of the room, shutting the door quickly before it explodes.

Whatever else happens, you may be sure that your guests will never return, and you can always demolish the remains of your room at will – or at the worst, use the squeegee to get it off the walls.

Cora Littledove's Main Chance

Wudgi Crossing in the spring is a pretty spot. When the first new shoots appear in the fields, and all of nature bursts into life; when the sun shines in a brilliant blue sky and the birds twitter in the trees, all seems right with the world. The people venture out from their cottages with a new spring in their step, and business picks up in the main street. The women get busy washing windows and changing curtains, while the men mow lawns and tidy up the gardens. It wasn't always like this!

In earlier days, Wudgi was more of a frontier town, with men outnumbering women by four or five to one. It was rugged in those days, rough, dirty and unrelieved by the deft touch of the fairer sex. Even as late as the 1960's, it was a predominantly male town, and any single woman had more offers than she could handle.

It's not generally known, but Mrs. Blithe-Brown of Progress Association fame, spent her younger years as a much sought after escort in Wudgi Crossing, long before she assumed the superior airs she displays today. As a young woman, Blithe-Brown, then known as Maude Clusterhumps, was a saucy little tease who was regularly involved in scandals and intrigues, relatively few of which came to the attention of the public.

She had a full date book, often going out with four or five fellows at the same time. It was great for the ego of a 22 year old, not so good for the four or five men involved. In fact, the younger of the fellows often came to blows over the situation, and Maude Clusterhumps was often in the middle of it.

"Now, now, don't you go fighting over little me," she would simper, then stand back and watch the sparks fly.

The staid matrons of the town, such of them as there were, did not view Maude in the most charitable of lights.

"Trollop," opined Mrs. Mopandle, Jim Mopandle's long-suffering mother. "Hussy," sniffed Mrs. Bill 'Rugged' Red, mother of Ralph 'Rough' Red, the town's larrikin. Mrs. Red didn't really have a leg to stand on if it were known, as she herself had been on more bicycle rides as a young girl than she would care to admit. Just the fact that she was married to 'Rugged' Red told the story, so the whispering tongues maintained.

Mrs. Littledove had more of a case, as her Cora

was a bit of a wallflower, and languished at home listening to the radio while Maude Clusterhumps froliced and disported herself among the male population like a hamper at a picnic. Everyone dipped into it.

"That girl will get herself into big trouble one day, you mark my words," said Mrs. Littledove, pursing her lips in distaste. "And my Cora can't even get a date!"

The fact that Cora had braces on her teeth and noticeably bowed spindly legs, of course, escaped her mother's attention. It was all Maude Clusterhumps' fault that the young males of the town took no notice of her Cora.

By the time Cora had reached her twenty-second birthday, still without a date, her mother was beginning to think that she would be saddled with her daughter forever. Cora made no effort to go out and meet people, but read lurid Romance magazines and Mills & Boon until her mother became quite desperate over the situation.

Then one day, a new face wandered into town. Peter Blithe was a charming young fellow of twenty six, who had been working in a Bank up north, and was now taking a spot of leave to travel and see a bit of the country. He booked into the

Wudgi Arms Hotel, and wandered about Wudgi Crossing introducing himself as he went. It was not long before he had met Jack Littledove, Cora's father, and was invited home for a meal.

Mabel Littledove saw her daughter's big chance, and bought Cora a new dress, gave her a stick of lipstick for the first time in her life, and a powder puff to take the sheen off her cheeks. Then she set up two candlestick holders on the table, and turned out the main lights to give a cosy, intimate atmosphere.

Cora had entered into the spirit of the thing by cooking up a big steak and kidney pie, as it was the one thing that she could do really well. Everyone who had ever tasted her pies had been effusive about how juicy they were, how tasty, and she should go into the pie business because she'd make a fortune.

When Peter Blithe sat down at the family table, Cora made her grand entrance, and sat opposite him, simpering. The only problem was that the powder had been somewhat overdone, and Cora looked like a corpse with a deathly pale complexion, and bright red lips that positively glowed in the candlelight. Every time she opened her mouth, the light reflected back off her braces, which her mother had forgotten to have removed on her sixteenth birthday.

Halfway through the meal, Mabel tugged at her husband's elbow and dragged him into the kitchen, so that the 'young folks' could get to know each other.

"But I haven't finished my pie," Jack complained in a loud whisper. "What about my pie?"

"There'll be hundreds of pies, Jack Littledove, but this might be the only time that anyone shows enough interest in your daughter's pie to take her off your hands. So shuttup!"

Jack shuttup, and helped himself to some apple pie and cream, standing by the kitchen sink to eat it.

Meanwhile, Peter Blithe was commenting on Cora's pie in the dining room.

"I say, this pie is simply scrumptious," he commented. "Did you make this pie?"

Cora nodded happily. He looked up and noted the white face and the red lips, caught a flash from her braces and was temporarily blinded. He adopted a look of concern.

"I do hope you're not sickening for something. You look very pale. You look as if you could do with another helping of pie yourself, get some colour in those cheeks."

"Oh, I never eat pie," said Cora. "I'm on a diet." What she really meant was: "I never eat pie because the pastry gets stuck in my braces."

"What? Nonsense my girl! You'll fade away to a shadow. Here, have some pie, put some meat on those bones, girl." He sliced a piece of pie off for her, and put it on her plate. She pulled a face.

"No, really. I can't break my diet. Isn't there anything else you like then, besides my pie?"

Cora pushed her chest out, and for the first time Peter saw how low-cut the dress was that her mother had bought for her. It was a shade this side of obscene. He flushed in confusion

"Oh, I like your br...usts," he stammered, his eyes popping out in surprise.

"I beg your pardon," Cora said, coyly, giving a little jiggle.

"Err... crusts, I like your pie crusts! Not soggy like so many pie crusts you come across. Very... er...firm, and – tasty! Well, they look tasty," he muttered, a mouth full of pie, and his eyes pinned on her twin mounds.

"I thought you said brusts," said Cora, "though you couldn't have, because there's no such thing.

Anyway, I said other than my pie..."

"Oh...oh... the mantle brust," he stammered, pointing at the mantlepiece. "Very fine, very nice brusts. I like your mantle brusts."

"I've never heard of a mantle brust," said Cora, puzzled and disappointed. "You don't mean the breastwork?"

"Oh, yes. Breastwork! Very good. Wouldn't mind a bit myself, actually."

"A bit of what," said Cora.

"Breast work. I've always worked in a Bank, you see. A bit of Breast work would be a nice change."

"There's no such thing," said Cora. "You're having a lend of me!" Then unaccountably she burst into tears. "I put on this dress especially for you, and you didn't even say nice things about my breasts."

Hearing her daughter cry, Mabel and Jack rushed into the room to find out what the matter was.

"What's he said to you, Cora? What's he said to upset you?"

At this the floodgates opened, and Cora howled.

"He said he liked the mantle brusts, and my pie crusts, and I've wriggled and wriggled and he hasn't said a word about my breasts."

Mabel looked at Peter, grimly.

"How could you be so unfeeling? The girl has put herself on display for you, and you can't even say something nice about her boobies."

"I... I...I..." said Peter, blushing and confused.

"What sort of a man are you," said Jack. "At the least you could have said you'd like a bit of a feel! I remember when I was courting her mother, why, I couldn't keep my hands off her breasts, could I Mabel. I was always..."

"Jack!" said Mabel, warningly. "We're talking about Cora here. What are your intentions, young man? You come here, invited into the pit of the family, and sit there gobbling Cora's pie, and not one word of encouragement for the poor girl. Not one lewd gesture, not one intimate foray into her cleavage! I must say, I'm surprised at you. Now Jack and I are going into the kitchen again, and if you haven't got yourselves onto that couch, and made considerable intrusions into Cora's underwear by the time we come back, then you're not the man we thought you were. Come on, Jack."

The two of them stalked off into the kitchen, and Cora moved over to the couch, and patted a place beside her. Peter swallowed the last piece of his pie, and looked nervously at her spindly legs. He got slowly to his feet and made as if to slouch over to the couch, then suddenly high-tailed it for the front door, and was through it and gone before Cora could yell for her parents.

The next day Jack caught up with Peter in the front bar of the Wudgi Arms. Far from being hostile, Jack threw his arm around Peter's shoulder, and patted him on the back.

"So here you are, you young devil. What have you been up to, you young gopher?"

Peter stood speechless, then took a swig of his Bundy and Coke.

"You've gotta watch this one," laughed Jack. "Quite the little lady killer, aren't you Peter?" The whole bar swung around to take notice of this. Things were looking interesting.

"Don't let him loose on your daughters," Jack continued, a smirk on his face. "Turn your back for a moment, and he's up to his armpits in their petticoats, aren't you Peter?"

Peter Blithe's jaw dropped, then he spun off his stool and headed for the door, blushing furiously.

"When are you coming back round for dinner – Cora's baking one of her steak and kidney pies tonight, lad," he yelled after him. There was a roar of laughter that followed Peter out into the street, where he stumbled straight into the arms of Maude Clusterhumps, of all people.

Maude had noted his arrival in the town, and had been quite put out by the fact that he had not, as yet, added himself to her bevy of admirers.

"Going somewhere, big boy," she intoned, fluttering her eyelashes at him.

"Yes, anywhere," he huffed, grabbing her by the arm. And that is how Maude ended up down on the banks of the creek, arm in arm with the new bad boy of the town, Peter Blithe.

Suddenly, Maude Clusterhumps lost interest in anyone but the new beau, and he in turn clung to her each time he saw a Littledove on the horizon. Exactly one month later, Maude Clusterhumps became Mrs. Blithe at the little Anglican Church in Wudgi Crossing, and Cora retreated to her radio, her Romance magazines and her Mills & Boon forever.

The union was a short-lived one. Peter Blithe was run over by a steamroller that accidentally mounted the footpath that summer, and rendered him as flat as a piecrust. Old Jack Littledove was devastated with remorse.

"I blame myself," he wept into his beer. "The roller just suddenly jumped up the kerb, and that young jacanapes – god, I loved him! – was sitting on the pavement reading his paper. All I heard was a sort of 'squrunch' – a bit like when you tuck into a good steak and kidney pie with a firm and tasty crust." Then he would burst into tears, howl a couple of times, then giggle like a little boy.

The constable eventually had to escort him up to the *Wudgi Sanatorium for the Criminally Insane*, just to give him time to get over his sad experience. Once there, a young Maude Sadismo took him under her wing, and promised to flush the butterflies and steamrollers out of his thoughts forever. The next time Mabel saw her husband, he had forsaken steak and kidney pies for bowls of sago, of which he thought he *was* one!

Cora continued her spinsterish life, and as she got older took to riding a three-wheeler up and down the main street, and into Fred Feeble's store, delivering her fabled steak and kidney pies. At these times she wore a dress cut away so steeply that you could see where the grand canyons got their name. Eventually, she made do with a telescope, and a chair by the window, to satisfy her vicarious urges.

The widow Blithe managed to marry a Duncan Brown within the year, but refused to part with her first husband's surname. She thus became Mrs. Blithe-Brown by default. But when, three months later, Duncan Brown died of food poisoning from one of the steak and kidney pies from Fred Feeble's shop, she decided that marriage just wasn't for her, and remained a widow for life.

Cora, in turn, never sold another pie in Wudgi Crossing.

Wallywools and the Pig Fest

Wudgi Crossing is not a large town. In comparison to Port Augusta, for instance, it is a blip on the road, a pimple on a bunion, a shag on a rock. Only during the annual Pig-Fest does Wudgi display any sense of having a population at all. At this time the town is packed with tourists, the creek banks overflow with campervans, the sidewalks are littered with empty Jim Beam bottles, and the woods are alive with giggles and squeals. It was at just such a Pig-Fest that Big Wal Wooly happened into town – I say happened, because in common with everyone else crowded together in the main street, he had actually been going somewhere else.

When he saw the lines of people snaking out from both Fred Feeble's store and the Fish and Chip shop, clutching Pig Pies and Bacon Pasties in bags, bottles of Raspberry, Lime and Lemon Pig in litres, and Pig-Burgers, Pig-Dogs, Pig on a Stick, and Pig and Chips, he rang up his mental cash register and said "Ping!!!"

Big Wal Wooly was the multimillionaire entrepreneur behind the Wallywool Stores, and he was said to have a knack for sniffing out the big bucks. He ran back to his car, pulled out a map and tried to locate Wudgi Crossing. He failed! Wudgi Crossing appears on no map made by man. Only the almighty has any real idea of where it is, and for the sake of humanity, he's keeping that information to himself.

Refusing to be beaten, Wal pulled out his mobile phone, and dialed a city number.

"Henry! Get a team of architects out here this minute; we're going to build a new store! At Wudgi Crossing!"

He listened to the voice on the other end for a moment.

"I know it's not on the map. No, I know we haven't done a feasibility study! Trust me – this place is humming."

The voice on the other end asked for directions.

"How the hell do I know? Just head for anywhere else, and you're bound to stumble across it. That's the way it works."

Ern Pigswill was in his element; it was his time of the year. Dressed in an ancient frock coat with frayed cuffs, a grey shirt with traces of pigslop down the front, and a pair of excrement encrusted boots, he was the master of ceremonies for the annual event. His chief pride and joy were his dancing pigs, and these held pride of place at the front of the procession.

He always dressed them up to resemble two notable characters in the town. This year it was the Mayor, 'Rough' Red, and the other was Mrs. Blithe-Brown. The latter wore a long gown and a little bonnet in the shape of a steamroller. Very bad taste, everyone agreed, but they laughed all the same. The 'Rough' Red Pig had a couple of bottles of plonk hanging from a fair imitation of a chain of office. He also had a top hat pinned precariously between his ears. Ralph roared uproariously when he saw it, took another swig from his own bottle and fell backwards into a horse trough.

The two pigs got up on their hind legs and swayed in time to "Old MacDonald's Farm', and everyone had a great time. Then Ern had his acrobatic troupe jumping through hoops, balancing on barrels, competing in a truffle hunt and taking kiddies for rides on Piggy carts.

At other venues around the town he had his 'Sheep-pigs' rounding up sheep in a paddock, his 'Bullock-pigs' pulling ploughs in concentric circles and his 'Ferret-pigs' routing out rabbits from rabbit holes. During the afternoon Ern's 'Clydesdale-pigs' drew huge drays up and down the main street, decked out in brightly coloured ribbons, the drays overloaded with beer barrels for the evening 'Pig-swill' that was such a feature of the event. The Wudgi Arms supplied the beer, and made a handsome profit on the proceedings, part of which was donated to the Pig-Fest Committee.

Those pigs without an especial talent were seen to be disinterestedly revolving slowly on spits all around the town for the giant Pig Picnic Fiesta, and these frivolities continued for a good ten days, long enough in fact, to destroy the most resilient liver.

Ern's Pig Farm was situated ten miles out of town, for obvious reasons. That hadn't always been so. His farm had once been situated at the bottom of the hill near the bridge, and when the wind came from a certain quarter, the smell had been enough to close down the main street for the day. It took twenty years of resident's complaints, twenty years of consultation with the council, and the odd death, due to massive olfactory malfunction, before the council finally agreed to swap the hundred acre block it owned out of town for the sixty acres of Ern's farm, just to get him away from the residential/business district.

Even then the smell didn't go away immediately. For years afterwards a good downpour would resurrect a steamy, midden-like mist from the affected area, which would creep up the hill and ambush the good citizens going about their daily business. At such times the Ambulance Crew was put on full alert and cruised up and down the hill, picking up unfortunate victims of the smell who had collapsed en route to and from their places of business.

Finally, after another fifteen years had elapsed, council sent the bulldozers in, scraped the surface of the ground, and piled the resultant smelly surface soil in a large square, some hundred yards back from the road. They then laid down a huge square slab of concrete over the whole, and the local lads used the resulting pad for roller-skating. The problem, they thought, was solved.

Wal Wooly fought his way through the crowds for the next three hours, looking for a likely place to build a Superstore. Coming to the bottom of the hill by the bridge he saw, in the distance, the concrete pad. It was presently occupied by campers and their trailers, but on further inspection he estimated it as being a hundred yards wide by sixty yards long, and immediately saw a way to save money. With the floor already in place, all he needed was four walls and a roof and he could be up and running in no time.

Wal never let the grass grow under his feet. Tracking down the Mayor, who was wallowing in an enclosure with a bottle of claret and two of Ern's Wrestling Pigs, he hauled him out and tried to bring him back to sobriety by dashing a pail of water in his face.

"I have important business, your worship. Get on your feet and meet me at the council offices."

There was consternation in the Wudgi Council Chambers the following day, where an emergency meeting had been called to discuss the urgent application of the Wallywool Stores to build a branch there.

"You can't let them in," protested Fred Feeble. "They'll suck every dollar out of the town, and everyone else will go broke."

"I disagree," said Jim Mopandle. "As President of the Progress Association, I would be derelict in my duty if I allowed an opportunity like this to pass us by. Just think of the people it will draw to the town. You'll have everyone from the outlying districts coming in to do their shopping, and they won't just go to Wallywool's. We'll even get the shoppers from Addlebury driving down to shop. Won't that be a coup?"

Ralph 'Rough' Red, the Mayor, his hands still shaking from the seventeen litres of Claret he had consumed the day before, banged his gavel in excitement.

"Yes, by god. We'll stick it to those Addlebury whackers once and for all. They got our Motel, but they're not going to get our Wallywools. Anyway, you will be delighted to know that yesterday, in the course of my, err... duties, I managed to sell off that crock of pigshit under that concrete block that we've been trying to work out what to do with for the past five years. This dork – err... that is, the entrepreneur, Mr. Wal Wooly, has bought it from the council for $50,000. That means, Fred, that you get a new verandah at no cost to yourself."

Fred looked somewhat mollified, and sat down. Everyone else applauded.

"No other objections? In that case, application passed!" said the Mayor.

The Pig-Fest went on for ten days. The architects and builders went to work amongst the milling throng at the bottom of the hill, and in three days had the sections airlifted in by helicopter, and the store up and running in four. Over two thousand people poured through the store on that first day, in various stages of inebriation. Wal Wooly stood by the checkouts and rubbed his hands together in appreciation every time a register went "Ping!"

Late in the afternoon, once the majority of the human effluent had dispersed, Wal wandered up to the rear of the store, and stopped to sniff the air. There was an unmistakable smell wafting up from the floor, and it wasn't pleasant.

"What's that god-awful smell," he asked the accountant.

"I don't know, but it's not good for a food shop. You'll have the health inspectors in here if it doesn't clear up."

The cleaners were put on the job, but the smell persisted. In fact, if anything, it got steadily worse! Wal sprayed various room deodorants around, and that masked it for the time being. But the concrete pad, being enclosed for the first time, exuded more of the foul smell overnight and bottled it up inside the building. When Wal threw the doors open the next day, the smell was enough to drop a bullock.

Worse than this, however, wandering nonchalantly down the middle of the store, and munching on a bunch of celery, was a small pig.

"How the blazes did a pig get in here," Wal exploded. He had the staff run around checking the entrances to make sure no door had been left unlocked overnight. The report came back that there was nowhere that a pig could possibly have got in, even a little one. The pig was shunted out of the store, and especial attention was paid to locking up that night. The following morning there were three more pigs, this time munching into the dress materials, the DVD rack, the fresh veg stand and the cake section. They'd left quite a trail of havoc behind them, and the smell was worse than ever.

It was then, and only then that Wal discovered the truth about the concrete pad. He called Ern Pigswill in for advice, and Ern told him the saga of his original farm.

"But what about these pigs – these little pigs I keep finding inside the store every morning. How are they getting in?"

Ern looked at Wal in surprise. "Is that right? It's true then! I always said it was funny, even back then. I used to get an extra sixty or seventy pigs a year like that."

"Like what?" Wal said, in exasperation.

"Spontaneous generation," Ern said, grandly. "Like mushrooms, you know? Pop up overnight."

Wal threw his hands in the air. "What claptrap! Spontaneous generation! I thought I was going to get some sense out of you."

"Well, just you figure it. There's about thirty years of pig dung under this block. It seeps up through the concrete and gives off a concentrated mist. You lock it up inside a building where it can concentrate more, and poof! - little pigs!"

Wal threw Ern out on his ear, and phoned the council offices.

"Now look here, Mayor. I bought this block of land in good faith, and now I find there's thirty years of pig manure under the floor, and the smell is bloody overwhelming. What are you going to do about it?"

'Rough Red' lay on the floor, his head in a bucket of ice. "Shmell? Mush be your buildersh! I's'll have t'send the Building Inshpector down t'have a look. But y'not shupposed to keep pigs in a food shop, y'know!"

"Pigs!" Wal yelled. "Yes, that's another thing. I've got pigs spontaneously generating overnight and chomping their way through the store."

Ralph pulled his head out of the bucket, and stared at the phone. "What *are* you talking about? Are you a Rosicrucian, or shomethin'?" Then he dropped the phone on the floor.

The Pig-Fest ran its course. Another thousand shoppers went through the store, and then, the next day, they all went home.

"Where the bloody hell is everybody," said Wal Wooly at lunchtime, scratching his head.

"I'm here," said Cora Littledove, riding in through the front doors on her three-wheeler. "Please direct me to the lens polishing cloths."

Cora peddled heroically up the aisle, but was turned back by a stampede of seven little pigs that appeared spontaneously from underneath the lay-by counter.

The Wudgi Wallywool Superstore had three customers that day, five the following day, and twenty seven day trippers from Addlebury on the Thursday. In that time another five immaculately conceived pigs were found truffling under the cash registers.

Wal Wooly surveyed his new store, checked out the seventeen new checkout operators standing dutifully at their posts, the fifteen shelf fillers running up and down the aisles, looking in vain for empty shelves to fill, and the five night cleaners sitting smoking outside the store, and went to his office to look for his Smith and Wesson .38.

"It's not that bad, Wal," said the accountant, looking up from his ledger. "Put that gun away and we'll consider our options."

The Wallywools Superstore was closed for a week, supposedly 'for alterations.' During that time the doors were shut tight, and no-one entered the store. At the end of that time one of the cleaners, Joe Yellowgums, a chain-smoking addict of 60 a day, was sent in to liberate whatever pigs had been spontaneously generated in the meantime. The atmosphere by then was almost pure methane, and even though Joe was provided with a suitable gas mask, he couldn't resist stopping in the middle of the store to light up another cigarette.

The explosion flattened all four walls simultaneously, and blew two million dollars worth of produce up into the stratosphere. The unfortunate Joe was the only human casualty. By some remarkable piece of providence he was shot into the overhead power lines, then catapulted back onto the roof of the Wudgi Arms Hotel. His only injuries were severely burned buttocks, and shrivelled black lips, where his cigarette had instantly imploded. He gave up smoking at that very moment, and has never been seen to inhale since.

Wal picked up a cool $7 million in insurance for his loss, and left the concrete pad to the young folk of Wudgi, to skate on or picnic on, or do whatever pleased them best. One thing is certain; Wudgi Crossing will never, ever again, be the site for a Wallywools Superstore. Just ask Wal!

www.ingramcontent.com/pod-product-compliance
Lightning Source LLC
Chambersburg PA
CBHW070445260626
47161CB00004B/1206